DARK OBSESSION

Determined to leave her old life behind and make a fresh start, Tory Matthieson takes her young daughter Millie and sets off into the unknown. Settling in the quiet village of Compton Cross, she makes new friends, including the handsome Damien Grey. But when a mysterious snooper appears, followed by a series of deeply disturbing events, Tory fears her past is catching up with her. Can she trust Damien to help her, when her last relationship ended so disastrously — and when they've only just met?

SUSAN UDY

DARK OBSESSION

Complete and Unabridged

LINFORD
Leicester

First published in Great Britain in 2017

First Linford Edition
published 2017

C463490263

A catalogue record for this book is available
from the British Library.

ISBN 978–1–4448–3223–5

Published by
F. A. Thorpe (Publishing)
Anstey, Leicestershire

Set by Words & Graphics Ltd.
Anstey, Leicestershire
Printed and bound in Great Britain by
T. J. International Ltd., Padstow, Cornwall

This book is printed on acid-free paper

1

The black-clad figure pulled the dark woollen hat low, before bending almost double and creeping noiselessly towards the illuminated window of the semi-detached house. It looked directly into a sitting room, where a group of small children were gathered. There were at least a dozen, and they were shouting and laughing as they darted madly around the room. Clearly, a birthday party was in progress.

The figure crept even closer, taking care to avoid the beam of light that shone outward into the garden. The tactic failed. One little girl's head turned towards the window, and she screamed, 'Daddy, Daddy, there's someone out there looking at us!'

The snooper did the only thing possible and retreated into the shadows that edged the small front garden, before ducking through the gateway to disappear along the unlit lane. Within seconds, there was no sign that anyone had ever been there.

★ ★ ★

'Have you heard? We seem to have some sort of peeping Tom in the village. He's been spotted several times over the past week, snooping through people's windows.'

Tory Matthieson stared at her friend Julia, her eyes wide with disbelief. 'A peeping Tom? Here in Compton Cross?' she scoffed. 'He'll very quickly run out of windows then. There can't be more than a hundred houses, if that. Are you sure it's not simply a case of imaginations running riot? January is a very boring month, after all, with its long, dark nights.'

'No. Ricky Harris was the last to see the culprit, and anyone less imaginative than him would be almost impossible to find. His little girl began shrieking, apparently. He managed to catch a glimpse of whoever it was before they ran off down Gypsy Lane. The person was wearing a hat pulled right down — presumably as a disguise. Whoever it was must have been up to no good, otherwise why hide his identity? His daughter said she saw scary eyes and they stared right at her.'

'It strikes me that, in contrast to her father, Ricky Harris's little girl *does* have an active imagination. If there was a peeping Tom, I'd have thought he would have picked somewhere bigger than a village to execute his dirty deeds. Less chance of being caught.'

'Well, I'm just repeating what I've heard.' Julia glanced across at her small daughter, who was clutching a doll to her chest and whining as she pushed her equally small companion away. 'Megan, share your toys, darling.'

'But it's my new doll, Mummy. The one Santa brought me.'

'Never mind that. You mustn't be self-ish. Santa wouldn't like that.'

'What time did these sightings take place?' Tory asked.

'Oh, about five-thirty, a couple a bit later.'

'In the afternoon, presumably?'

'Well, it wouldn't be the morning, would it?'

'No, but it's a bit early to be snooping through people's windows, wouldn't you say? High risk of being caught — as he very nearly was.'

'Ricky did say he wondered if whoever it was could have been looking for someone in particular. According to his daughter, he looked right round the room, from child to child.'

Tory felt a shiver of apprehension — fear, even. 'Looking for someone?'

'Yeah. Searching, not just staring.'

Tory swallowed nervously. 'What did he look like? Tell me again.'

Julia regarded her anxiously. 'Are you all right? You've gone very pale.'

'I'm fine. Just tell me what Ricky said.'

'Not much, really. He couldn't see the face properly because of the hat. He did say the person wasn't very tall. And like his daughter, when the man briefly glanced backwards, he especially noticed the eyes. They were — now, how did he

4

describe them? — oh yeah, they were piercing and definitely blue.'

'Blue?'

'Yeah. And he also mentioned the menacing look he had. I think it unnerved Ricky a bit. He's reported it to the police, anyway.'

'Okay. Right — that's good. Good.' She glanced across at Millie, her daughter, unable to extinguish her feeling of misgiving.

Julia asked again, 'Are you all right, Tory?'

Tory's smile was a shaky one now. She told herself she was overreacting, seeing shadows where none existed. She had to stop this. After almost six months, she and Millie were settled here. She'd made friends, good friends; they both had. She'd made a new life for them, just as she'd wanted. She mustn't allow her fears to destroy it. They were safe. If anything was going to happen to endanger that, it surely would have happened by now — wouldn't it?

Pulling herself together, she smiled

warmly at Julia. Her friend was watching, her expression a troubled one. 'It was probably a tramp, hoping for a hot meal and a bed somewhere.'

'You're right,' Julia agreed, unable to hide her relief at her friend's swift recovery. 'That's much more likely. But ...'

Tory regarded her warily.

'Wouldn't he have just knocked on the door if that were the case?'

* * *

Once Tory had left Julia's house and driven back to her own semi-detached cottage with Millie — for once, she'd used her car rather than walking, because it had been such a wet, miserable morning — she swiftly went round the house, making doubly sure that the doors, front and back, were locked, and that all the windows were securely fastened. Maybe she was being overly cautious, but it was wiser, nonetheless, to take a few sensible precautions.

'Mummy,' Millie said as Tory bathed

her and got her ready for bed, 'what's a peeping Tom? Is it a sort of cat?'

'No, darling. It's someone who likes to spy on other people and see what they're doing.'

'A nosy parker then?'

Tory laughed. For a three-year-old, Millie was at times remarkably perceptive. 'You're right. A nosy parker is the perfect description.'

Millie frowned then. 'Will he look through our windows? 'Cos I wouldn't like that.'

'I'm sure he won't.'

'Why are you sure?'

'I just am, especially if we draw the curtains each evening. And, after all, we aren't that interesting, are we?'

Millie took her time in considering that observation before saying, 'Mrs Jenkins says that I've got a very int'resting way with words.'

'She might be right!' Tory laughed, clasping her daughter close to her.

Mrs Jenkins was one of the three women who ran the local nursery school;

in fact, she was the one in charge. She was a good-natured, sensible and eminently patient woman, always finding time to listen to a small child's comments and observations. Millie and Megan attended the group three days a week. Tory had every faith in her ability to take good care of Millie. As Tory worked on one of the checkouts in a small mini-market in the village five days a week, Julia took care of Millie the rest of the time. It wasn't the job Tory had hoped for, but it had been the only one she could find at the time. She'd been trained for secretarial work, which she'd had to give up once she had Millie.

But nowadays, as a single parent, she needed an income and so had gladly accepted the job. And, in truth, she enjoyed it. So much so, that she was in no hurry to find anything else. It was relatively stress-free, a state of mind she'd been sorely in need of when she first arrived in Compton Cross almost six months ago. In addition, it provided her with the opportunity to meet people, lots of people, and thus make friends. And, as she'd told herself at the time, beggars couldn't be choosers.

It had been how she'd met Julia, and they'd swiftly become good friends. Now, Tory didn't know what she'd do without her. It had been Julia who'd cheered her in her lowest moments; Julia, who never asked awkward questions. It was as if she sensed Tory's reluctance to confide and had readily accepted her reticence.

She tucked the duvet tightly round her daughter and dropped a kiss onto the smooth, round cheek. The little girl was almost asleep already. 'Night-night, my precious. Don't let the bed bugs bite.'

Without opening her eyes, Millie chuckled. 'Silly Mummy, we don't have bed bugs.'

'I know. Aren't we lucky?'

Millie's eyes suddenly snapped open. 'Mummy, when are we going to see Daddy?' An anxious expression briefly darkened the little girl's eyes.

'I don't know, darling. Daddy's very busy. Now, go to sleep.'

Millie popped her thumb into her mouth. 'Okay. Night-night, Mummy.'

'Good girl.' And she dropped another kiss onto her daughter's cheek.

Once Tory was back in the sitting room, she put a match to the paper and kindling that was already laid in a log burner, before, in an effort to distract herself from her steadily growing unease, turning on the television. She told herself that there was nothing to worry about; the peeping Tom had likely been a tramp. And if he showed up at her cottage, he'd get very short shrift indeed. But, just to make sure, she went to the window that looked out onto the road and drew the curtains. Then, feeling fractionally more confident, she glanced around the room that was now home.

The cottage wasn't a large one; in fact, it was small — compact, as the agent had described it — but it was comfortable and contained all she and Millie needed. She'd rented it furnished, which was just as well because she hadn't been able to bring anything much with her; a few clothes for each of them, and, of course, Millie's toys. They'd even had to leave a few of those behind — much to Millie's dismay. But she simply hadn't got room for a doll's house, a doll's stroller and a rocking horse.

She recalled the day they'd set off. She hadn't had a clue as to where they were going. She'd put her and Millie's suitcases into the boot of her Fiesta, and filled the back seat with toys — Millie's car seat was in the front — and had just driven. They'd left Warwickshire, where they'd lived until then, and headed west. Wales, she'd vaguely decided. A new life, somewhere among the hills and mountains.

She didn't make it quite that far, however.

Upon spotting the sign for Compton Cross and dimly recalling driving through it years ago with her parents on their way to Wales for a holiday, she decided to go and have a look. It would only be a few miles out of her way, and, if she remembered it correctly, it had been very pretty, and more importantly, very much of a backwater. She'd easily been able to envisage making her new life there. So, she'd turned the car off the main road and driven in that direction.

But it turned out to be further than she'd remembered, and she certainly hadn't remembered the series of tortuous lanes that led to it. Still, the journey had proved worthwhile. The village, larger than she recalled, had still been every bit as pretty. She'd passed a small church, a library, a couple of pubs. There was even a rather smart-looking café, and a bistro restaurant. She'd parked on the roadside in the main street and found a tiny estate agency sandwiched between a butcher's and a greengrocer's, where she asked if they had anything available to rent immediately. They had, and so here they were, comfortably settled in Primrose Cottage. The initial rental payment had made a sizable hole in the money she'd brought with her, but that hadn't mattered at the time. The important thing was they'd had somewhere to live.

* * *

That night, Tory dreamed. She was being pursued across a field. It was deep with mud and her feet kept being sucked down, until it felt as if she were struggling through treacle. And all the time, her pursuer was closing in on her. He got so close, she could hear his rasping breath, feel it on the back of her neck. She looked behind. He was dressed all in black, with a woollen hat pulled well down over his face. Piercing blue eyes stared back at her from beneath the brim; they were filled with hatred.

'I'm coming for you,' he growled. 'You won't escape.'

She woke suddenly, a scream tearing up her throat.

'Mummy!' she heard Millie cry. The little girl sounded as frightened as Tory had just been. 'Mummy, come quickly — please. Ple-ease.'

Tory leapt from her own bed and ran into her daughter's room, which overlooked the road. Millie was standing in front of her window, the curtains pulled back to reveal the darkness of the night. Her small face was white, her eyes wide and terrified as she looked up at her mother.

Tory ran to her and picked her up. 'It's okay, darling. It was just Mummy having a bad dream. Ssh, ssh.' She rocked the child, trying to calm her.

'Can I sleep with you?' Millie asked through deep sobs. 'I'm frightened. I heard a loud bang outside, and I looked out, and someone was there. Is it the peeping Tom?'

'No, my precious. I'm sure it wasn't. You were dreaming too.'

But had she been? Could she have heard something outside, something that had driven her to pull back the curtains and look out? Had she, in fact, spotted the snooper?

'He looked up at me, Mummy. He did. He waved. I saw him.'

Tory went to the window. It was a heavily clouded night, which meant there were no stars, no moon, nothing to illuminate the road below. Even the street lights were off — not that there were many of those in this quiet side road. But, even so, she could see that there was no one out there. She breathed a small sigh of relief. It must have been her and Julia's conversation about the snooper that had given Millie her nightmares. 'There's no one out there, sweetie. It was a nasty dream. But you can sleep with me, just this once.' And she carried the little girl through to her own room.

It was as she was climbing into bed alongside her daughter that, with a sickening lurch of her heart, she realised she'd left her car on the drive instead of putting it into the garage as she normally did. Which meant that if the snooper was who she thought it might be, and had been outside as Millie insisted, then her car would have been instantly recognised, and her and Millie's whereabouts would be known.

★　★　★

The next morning, they were both heavy-eyed and pale from lack of sleep. Millie had tossed and turned all night, flinging arms and legs wide, keeping Tory awake in the process. But it hadn't just been Millie who'd deprived her of sleep. Tory's own reflections — mainly her deep dismay at her carelessness in leaving her car outside — had also done their bit. She could only hope that her fears would turn out to be misplaced.

But no matter how she felt, she had to go to work. She dressed Millie in her play clothes, disregarding the small girl's grumbling that she didn't want to go to Julia's that day. 'I want to stay at home with you, Mummy,' she said.

'You can't, Millie. I have to go to work. And it's very kind of Auntie Julia to take care of you.' Especially as Julia adamantly refused to take any money from Tory. Tory had tried to insist but Julia had said, 'No, Tory. If I can't help out a friend it's a pretty poor show. Anyway,' she glibly went on, 'my alimony keeps me very well. That's one thing I can't grumble about.

Dan's very generous. Guilty conscience, I suppose.' She'd sniffed her contempt for her ex-husband. 'But then again, why shouldn't he pay up for what he did to me?'

It had been before Tory arrived in Compton Cross that Julia had discovered her husband had been having an affair for two years. He'd subsequently left to live with the other woman, and Julia had wasted no time in divorcing him. The whole episode had left her very bitter, and determined to never place herself at the mercy of another man. Though she did depend entirely upon Dan for her income, Tory reflected with a wry smile. Anyway, it meant she was free to care for Millie while Tory worked, for which Tory was truly thankful. There was no one she trusted more with her daughter.

She dropped Millie off on her way to the mini-market; it was situated at the far end of the main street, next door to the library. Neither Julia's house nor the mini-market was far from Primrose Cottage, which meant she could walk there and back, and so cut down on her motoring costs. In fact, she was beginning to question whether she really needed a car anymore. Selling it would go some way towards improving her financial situation, which always seemed to be tricky. And whatever money she got for it would be very welcome at the moment. An electric bill was due at any time. And Millie was soon going to need some new shoes, as well as a new coat, so quickly was she growing.

It was a frosty morning, the coldest of the winter so far, and the pavements were slippery. Which must have been why, as she was approaching the shop, her feet slid from beneath her; before she could do anything to save herself, she was falling. As she hit the ground backwards and her head slammed on the hard pavement, she quietly moaned, closing her eyes as she did so.

'Oh, good Lord,' she muttered, before opening them once more to find herself staring up into the disturbingly handsome features of a complete stranger.

'Well,' he murmured, his unusual walnut-coloured eyes gleaming as he regarded her, 'this is a first. A beautiful maiden literally falling at my feet, and at this time of the morning to boot.'

2

Tory glared up at him. Not only did she deeply resent the sexist nature of his remark, but she also felt extremely foolish.

He didn't look the slightest bit bothered by her expression of outrage, and instead of apologising he coolly asked, 'Can I help you up?' before holding out a noticeably well-cared-for hand. But his politeness was clearly nothing more than a front, because despite his level tone, his eyes continued to gleam at her — with amusement, she furiously concluded.

So he found her predicament funny, did he? Well, here was a newsflash: it wasn't funny; not funny at all. She could very well have broken something, falling onto the icy ground as she had. Pointedly ignoring his hand, she gingerly moved. However, nothing felt broken. Nothing even felt hurt — apart from her pride, of course. And that was well and truly injured.

'Come on, please,' he coaxed, 'let me help you. I saw you go down, and you landed with quite a thump. You might have damaged something.'

Grudgingly, Tory did as he asked and grasped the proffered hand. Just as she'd expected, it was perfectly smooth and warm and very strong, as with little or no effort at all, as far as she could detect, he hauled her to her feet. Yet she'd stake her life on the fact that those well-kept hands had never done a day's labour in their life.

'Thank you,' she rather ungraciously muttered.

'You're welcome.' The maddening gleam was still there in those unusually coloured eyes. 'Now, does everything feel okay? All still working? How about your head?'

'I'm fine.' And she was, even if the aforementioned head did throb a little. However, she wasn't about to tell him that, because he'd probably find that amusing too. Instead she glanced down over herself and saw that her skirt, which already ended a couple of inches above her knees, had now ridden halfway up her thighs. Hence the gleaming eyes? Quickly she tugged it down and looked back up at her rescuer.

It was then that she felt her breath catch in her throat. He was far too good-looking for comfort. Tall, six feet one or two inches, she estimated — he certainly dwarfed her five feet five inches — with a powerful physique clearly visible beneath the coat he was wearing. His thick, tawny-coloured hair reached half-way down the back of his neck, an almost exact match for his eyes; a lock of hair had even managed to drop attractively forward onto his forehead, increasing his already stunning good looks. Quite irrationally, that just made her all the angrier. His nose was Grecian — of course it was, she shouldn't have expected anything less; his cheekbones were perfectly sculptured; his mouth ... She drew another breath. His mouth was unashamedly sensuous, with its full lower lip. If you added a chis-elled jawline to all of this, you ended up with a man so handsome he could have graced a cinema screen.

'Are you sure?' His voice was throaty and, it seemed to Tory, provocatively seductive.

So much so, she was tempted to say, 'No, will you help me?' Instead, she coolly replied, 'I'm all right, really. A trifle shaken, that's all.'

'Can I take you anywhere? My car's parked just here.' He indicated a black Range Rover — a top-of-the-range model, naturally — parked at the kerbside.

She only just stopped herself from snorting her scorn out loud. These men and their big, expensive cars. They were nothing more than an extension of their oversized egos.

'No need,' she said. 'I work just here.' She pointed to the mini-market a few metres further along the road. 'Thank you for the offer, though.' She was sure that simply driving her the short distance necessary would consume more fuel than her car would use in an entire week.

He glanced at the frontage and then back at her. Then he proceeded to eye her, his expression one of undisguised curiosity now. 'What do you do there?'

'I work at one of the checkouts.'

He made no attempt to hide his surprise at that. She felt a pang of annoyance, and then to her chagrin heard herself trying to justify her choice of work. 'I've only lived here for a few months. It was all I could find, and I needed a job.' Her words petered out beneath his piercing stare.

'What did you do before you came here?'

'I was a secretary to an MD in a ...'

'Bit of a waste of your ability, wouldn't you say? To sit at a checkout?' he impertinently cut in.

He was scrutinising her intently now, and although heavy lids veiled his eyes, she thought she detected a hint of scorn. A further explosion of indignation, at his manner as well as his words, went off inside her. Who the hell did he think he was, criticising her choice of job?

Despising it even, and furthermore, making no attempt to hide that judgement.

'Not really,' she spoke sharply. 'It's helped me make a lot of friends, good friends, which I wouldn't have done if I'd been penned up in an office.'

'Well, that's one way of looking at it, I suppose.' He was still studying her, his gaze a penetrating one.

Tory started to fidget.

'Well, if you ever want to broaden your horizons and use that ability, let me know. I'm sure I can find you something a bit more challenging.'

She stiffened at the look in his eye. What the hell did he mean, more challenging? As what? She had no wish to return to secretarial work. She suspected she'd find working in the confines of an office smothering now. Despite his evident scorn, she was perfectly happy sitting at a checkout.

She noticed he was appraising her. If the expression in his eyes was anything to go by, she wouldn't be the least bit surprised if he offered her the position of his mistress. His gaze moved lazily down over her shapely legs in their black tights and ankle boots, before lifting once again to her face and the hazel eyes that could look green in certain lights; to her pert, lightly freckled nose; her high cheekbones; her full, naturally rose-tinted lips; and finally the cloud of curly hair, the exact shade of a horse chestnut, which reached down her back to end just beneath her shoulders. It was so thick, and there was such an abundance of it, that really she needed to pin it up in some sort of a loose knot. But no matter how much hair lacquer she applied, it never stayed that way for any length of time. Wavy strands would swiftly work loose and curl lovingly around her ears and the sides of her face. She'd long since given up trying for neatness and sophistication, and now left it to more or less go its own way.

'I'm always on the lookout for good people,' he murmured.

'Are you?' Her lips tightened. 'I'll keep that in mind; not that I'm considering any sort of move at the moment.' And he'd be the last type of man she'd choose to work for. She'd seen enough of his sort; had her fill of them, in fact. Too good-looking, too arrogant, too full of themselves — too much of everything. Like Julia, she'd had enough of men, period. The pair of them were better off on their own.

Undaunted by her coolness, he slid a hand into an inside pocket and pulled out a card, which he thrust at her. She took it, mainly out of curiosity. She read: 'Damien Grey, Grey Enterprises', followed by a number with a local code. There was also the number of a mobile phone.

'You can reach me any time on either of those numbers. The mobile is my private number.'

She glanced at him. 'You live locally?'

'Yes. At Compton Court.'

Wow! Compton Court was a huge place; a manor house, in actual fact. She'd been doing some reading just lately on the history of this area, and had discovered that four centuries ago Compton Court had been the home of the Compton family, the aristocratic owners of most of the village at the time. Over the next couple of hundred years, large parts of the land and the village were gradually sold off to subsidise the extravagant habits of the owners and their descendants. However, the house, mainly untouched, still sat regally in the centre of many acres of land and ornamental gardens, and the whole was enclosed by high hedges. A gated driveway guaranteed total privacy for the occupants. Not that she'd ever been inside either the house or the grounds, but she had glimpsed it from the road while driving past. Strangely, nobody had ever actually mentioned who now owned it.

She'd deliberately slowed down on one occasion, her curiosity getting the better of her, and had been able to see that it was a very impressive building, with a steeply sloping grey slate roof decorated with an inordinate number of ornamental chimney pots; it had silvery grey stone walls punctuated with rows of mullioned and leaded windows. The finishing touch to this display of magnificence was a grandly colonnaded entrance.

She should have guessed, she decided now, from the way this man was behaving and talking with what was beginning to look like an innate self-assurance, that there was a very good chance he was the owner of such a magnificent house. It smacked of wealth and power, as did he. Maybe he was a descendant of the original owners and fancied himself as an aristocrat still?

'Thank you,' she said, 'but I doubt I'll ever need to reach you.' She only just managed to stop herself from blurting out, 'Why on earth would I?' Sadly, biting her tongue was something she was frequently forced to do, as from the age of eight or nine it had developed the maddening habit of running away with itself. This had landed her in deep trouble more than once. In fact, it had lost her a job a few years earlier. It had also almost got her expelled from school on a couple of memorable occasions. Fortunately, she seemed to be in better control of its waywardness nowadays — well, most of the time, at any rate.

'Do you have a card?' he asked.

She stared at him. Did she look like the sort of woman who'd have a card? Tory Matthieson, till-operator in the Harrison Mini-market? She only just stopped herself from laughing out loud. 'No, I don't.'

He cocked his head to one side. 'What's your name?'

'Tory; Tory Matthieson.'

'Tory?' He raised an eyebrow. 'That's unusual.'

'Is it? Not to me.'

Amusement glittered in his eyes and lightly quirked the corners of his mouth. Again, her breath snagged in her throat. No man had the right to be so impossibly handsome. She wouldn't mind betting he had women chasing him all over the place. Or maybe he was married? She'd put money on him not being faithful, if he was. Although she noticed he wasn't wearing a ring.

'Where do you live?' he went on to ask.

'Here — in Compton Cross.'

'Yes, I've already worked that out for

myself, as you're clearly walking to work.' There was a trace of ironic humour both in his voice and expression.

He was the most irritating man, making such an assumption. She could have parked somewhere nearby. He clearly hadn't considered that. And why did he care where she lived? They'd probably never meet again. They were hardly likely to mix in the same social circles. Despite that, she heard herself saying, 'Chester Road.' Then, giving in beneath his air of expectation, she added, 'Number twenty-two.'

'Well, Tory Matthieson, if I hear of any jobs going begging, I'll let you know.'

'There's no need to trouble yourself; I'm perfectly happy where I am.'

'It can't pay much, though. Let me have your phone number. I'll put it into my mobile.'

For heaven's sake, was there no stopping this man? He'd be demanding to know what she did for recreation next, or what she ate for dinner; what time she went to bed. Nonetheless, to her utter disgust, she meekly told him her mobile number, not the landline. She almost never used that, and he wouldn't be able to find it in the phone directory; her name wouldn't be entered until the next edition was issued, which was probably several months away. But then she compounded her weakness by blurting, 'I have a daughter.' Good grief, was there nothing she wasn't prepared to tell him?

Again he raised an eyebrow, the same one. Who did he think he was, Roger Moore? This time she did snort her amusement — only softly, but it was still unmistakably a snort.

Anyway, he couldn't have heard her indiscretion because he smoothly asked, 'It's just you and her, is it?'

She nodded.

'Well, maybe you'd like to come out one evening?'

'She's too young to bring.'

He grinned, really grinned, flashing a set of perfectly even teeth at her. The simple gesture transformed his features into mind-blowing attractiveness. 'I wasn't asking you to bring her. I had just you and I in mind, not a threesome. Oh!' He grinned abashedly, as he realised what he'd said. His grin broadened even further as the warmth of a blush fanned the skin of Tory's face.

'No, I don't think so, thank you.'

'Sorry.' He grimaced ruefully. 'I don't know why I said that. I'm quite harmless, really. Oh, and in case you were wondering, I'm single too. Never been married.'

That surprised her. He must be at least in his mid-thirties. Why was a man this good-looking still alone?

'I can't leave my little girl. She's only three.'

'There are such things as babysitters,' he retorted.

'I don't see enough of her as it is, what with working full-time. And with our recent move, she's still a bit ... insecure. Look, I must get to work.'

He disregarded her last few words and instead asked, 'Insecure? Why's that?'

That's none of your business, she felt like saying, but again she bit her tongue.

'She's had a bit of a difficult time.'

'Okay, but I won't pretend I'm not disappointed.'

And, she conceded, he did look it. Surely he couldn't be interested in her? He must have women waiting in line for him. Why on earth was he asking her out? Okay, she admitted she was reasonably attractive, but that was all. Reasonably. She was never going to win any sort of beauty contest.

'Well, maybe some other time?' He didn't miss a beat.

Intrigued, despite everything she'd just been thinking about him, she eyed him.

'And,' he went on, 'if you should change your mind, you have my card.'

She made a point of glancing at her wristwatch then, and saw that she should have been at work five minutes ago. Naturally he wouldn't consider that, being his own boss presumably. He clearly expected everyone he encountered to accommodate his demands — certainly not to be forced himself to accommodate someone else's. And that reflection only served to intensify Tory's exasperation with him. She gnawed at her lower lip.

'I must go. My manager is a stickler for good time-keeping. I'll be getting the sack at this rate.'

'In that case, call me.'

He was impossible, she concluded. Give him an inch, she suspected, and he'd grab the whole damn mile. She hurriedly walked away, trying her best not to limp. As it turned out, she did seem to have hurt her ankle slightly. If he should glance back at her, she wouldn't put it past him to insist on taking her home. She couldn't quite suppress her feeling of satisfaction, though, at the fact that she'd somehow managed to capture the interest of such a handsome, charismatic and, by all appearances, wealthy man. Even so, she wasn't remotely tempted to meet up with him. What on earth would they have to talk about? They'd have absolutely nothing in common. In fact, he was so far out of her world, he might as well be an alien.

* * *

It was almost a week later that Tory was awoken by a sound downstairs. Only a faint one; but in the wake of Julia's tale of a possible peeping Tom, and her own suspicions as to his identity, she was instantly alert. She levered herself up in bed on one elbow and listened intently. It had sounded like a cupboard door closing. She squinted at her clock, which sat on the bedside table, and saw that it was eleven forty-five. She hadn't been asleep long.

She swung her legs out from beneath the duvet and crept into Millie's room. But Millie lay on her back, sleeping soundly. Clearly, nothing had disturbed her. Tory glanced around the room. All was as it should be. Nonetheless, she couldn't leave things like that. She went out of the room and soundlessly descended the stairs. When she reached the bottom she stood still, once again listening. Nothing; no sound at all.

She crept into the kitchen. At first glance, everything looked as it should

— and then she belatedly noticed the window. It was open, and swinging back and forth as a breeze caught it. She hurried across and closed it. Had she left it like that? She was sure she hadn't. She glanced around at all the cupboard doors. They were closed.

She couldn't stop herself then. She went to each one and opened it, carefully inspecting the contents. All of them seemed as she'd left them — except for one. The last one. She stared. She was sure she hadn't left it like that.

Cans of soup were lined up in a perfect row. The same thing had been done with cans of beans and tomatoes. Packets of rice had been placed upright, one stiffly balanced against the next.

She frowned. Could she have done this? If she had, she didn't have any memory of it at all. It was the sort of thing Stuart would have done. Her heart missed a beat. She chewed at her bottom lip. If she hadn't left her car on the driveway last night, and Millie hadn't said she'd seen someone outside, Tory wouldn't be thinking like this. She was reading more into it than she should. If Stuart had been here, how would he have got in? No, it must have been her. She'd got so used to keeping everything in order that she'd probably done it without thinking. Nonetheless, she checked the kitchen door that led into the garden — it was securely locked. Then she went to the front door, but that was firmly closed as well. With a heart that was stilling beating far too fast for comfort, she went into the sitting room. A swift glance round showed her that everything was exactly as she'd left it.

For heaven's sake, she was becoming paranoid. Just because Julia had briefly mentioned a snooper. She tried to reason things through calmly and rationally. There was no evidence of a break-in, other than the kitchen window. But that hadn't been smashed, which it would have to have been for someone to open it from outside and climb in. Yet there were still those items in the cupboard, arranged so neatly, so meticulously in order.

Eventually she succeeded in convincing herself that she'd been the one responsible for it all, no one else, and she returned to bed.

3

Against all her expectations, Tory slept, dreamlessly and soundly; so soundly, in fact, that it took Millie crawling in beside her the next morning to wake her. Tory hugged her small daughter to her and sighed happily as she plastered kisses all over the softly rounded cheeks. It was Saturday and she'd booked the day off. So no work, no rush.

'Tell you what,' she said. 'Let's go to the zoo.' There was a small one just a couple of miles away from them. It wasn't strictly a zoo, just a collection of farm animals that children had access to, allowing them to pet and feed them and thus get to know them. Millie loved it there.

'Yeah,' she sang now. 'We're going to the zoo!'

Tory organised their breakfast — boiled eggs and toast for Millie, scrambled eggs for her — and by eleven o'clock they were on their way. She'd phoned Julia, and she and Megan were joining them. Tory picked them up in her car, and soon they were walking through the gates towards the animal pens.

It was a cold day with a cloudless blue sky and a bright winter sun. And when a robin sang from a nearby hedgerow and the scent of woodsmoke drifted through the still air towards them, Tory decided this was just what she needed. It would banish her ridiculous night-time panic, because the more she considered her suspicions about Stuart, the more im-probable they seemed to be. The snooper, peeping Tom, whatever he was, was just that — a snooper. She mustn't read any more into it. Just as she mustn't read any-thing into her tidy cupboards. She herself must have done it, acting out a habit that had become second nature to her.

'What a great idea this was,' Julia said. 'Just what the doctor ordered.'

'Are you sick?' Tory asked in some concern.

'Yeah, sick of my life.'

Tory's heart sank. 'Oh, is it too much for you, having Millie?'

'God, no, don't be daft. I love having her. So does Megan. No, it's not that. I suppose I'm bored, truth be known. I don't seem to do anything. And to be honest, housework isn't exactly fulfilling. I've been thinking of getting a job.'

Tory regarded her in dismay.

'Oh, don't worry. It would only be part-time. I could still have Millie.'

What was it with Julia? Tory asked herself. At times, she seemed to have the uncanny knack of reading Tory's mind. Not about everything, thank goodness. There were some things she didn't want her friend to know.

'Of course, she and Megan might have to go a little bit more often to the nursery — at least for part of the day.'

Which, frankly, wasn't very reassuring to Tory. It would cost her money that she simply didn't have. Unless she sold the Fiesta? But if she did that, she wouldn't be able to bring Millie to places like this. 'What would you do?'

Julia shrugged. 'Dunno. That's the problem.'

'I was told I was wasting my talents the other day.'

Julia stared at her. 'Who by?'

'Damien Grey.'

'Damien Grey! How the hell did you meet Damien Grey?'

'I literally fell at his feet.' She recalled his description of her — a beautiful maiden — and couldn't help but smile. The phrase conjured up an image of a sixteen-year-old girl, not the twenty-seven-year-old woman and mother that she was. Maybe she should have found it flattering, rather than taking offence.

'You what?' Julia was regarding her with amazement.

'I trod on a patch of ice, slipped and fell flat — not very gracefully, I might add — right in front of him.'

'Wow! Did he pick you up?'

'More or less. He asked me what I did, I told him, and he said I was wasting my talents; that he could find me something more challenging to do, which I thought

43

was a bit of a cheek. There's nothing wrong with manning a checkout. And if he did but know it, it's very challenging some of the time, especially when Mrs Foster comes in.' She pulled a wry face. 'She's always flippin' whinging about something. Not enough staff, she has to queue too long, or she can't find exactly what she wants. God, the wretched woman never stops!'

Julia chuckled. 'I know who you mean. I've heard her in other shops. She seems to think it's her role in life to make everyone else as miserable as she is. But go on, I'm all ears. What did he have in mind for you? Private secretary to him?' Julia eyed her, almost jealously at that point. 'You want to watch yourself. He's acquired quite a reputation with women. Mind you, I've seen him a couple of times around and about, and I wouldn't mind a go at him.' She widened her eyes lustfully. 'He's bloody gorgeous — excuse my French. I wonder,' she added, sounding excited all of a sudden, 'do you think he could find a job for me? I'd do his typing any day of the week.' She growled, cat-like.

'I'm sure you would, but behave yourself. Little ears are listening. Anyway, do you know where he lives?'

'Yeah. Compton Court.'

'You've never mentioned it.'

'Never thought about it. And you didn't ask, so why would I?' Julia regarded her quizzically.

'Good point.'

'Why don't you let him find you something? Could be worth your while. It would certainly mean more money.'

'No way. I intend to keep my distance from handsome men nowadays.' She bit at her lower lip. She hadn't meant to say that.

Julia's curiosity was instantaneous — just as she'd feared. 'You've never told me anything about Millie's father. And I haven't liked to ask. But … you're obviously not together.'

'No, we're separated.'

'What happened?'

'Oh, you know. We weren't compatible. It seemed best to call it a day.'

'But you were married?'

Tory looked nervously at Millie. She hoped she wasn't listening to this. But the little girl was happily engrossed in petting a goat. 'Yes, we were married.'

'Do you ever hear from him?'

'No.'

'He doesn't see Millie, then?'

'No. It's better this way.' She was beginning to sound defensive, she realised. Time to put an end to this particular discussion before Julia pressed for even more details. She called to the children: 'Who wants an ice cream?'

Julia must have realised what Tory was doing, but, displaying uncharacteristic restraint, she offered no argument — although she did look more than a tad frustrated.

From the zoo, they went on to a nearby town, larger by far than Compton Cross, where they found a MacDonald's and proceeded to gorge themselves on burgers and fries. Tory decided to make the most of the opportunity and purchase a few things for Millie that she hadn't been able to buy in the village, after which, slightly wearily, they returned to Julia's.

'Come in and have a cup of tea,' she invited. 'The kids can watch TV for a bit and we can have a natter.'

But Tory knew full well what that meant. Julia, her curiosity well and truly aroused, would relentlessly pump her for more information about her marriage. And that was the last thing that Tory wanted at this particular moment.

'Thanks, Julia, but I've got loads to do at home.'

'Like what?'

'Like a pile of ironing and more washing.' She gave an exaggerated groan. She had no intention of doing either. They could wait until tomorrow, but it had been the only excuse she could think of on the spur of the moment.

'Spoilsport,' her friend muttered. 'Can't all that wait? I'll open a bottle of wine.' She wiggled her eyebrows. 'We can have a bit of a party.'

'No, really. As tempting as it sounds, I must go.'

Julia sighed and climbed out of the front passenger seat. 'Okay. I can't argue with such dedication. Come on, Megan. Looks like it's just you and me.'

Tory felt bad then. Megan began to whine, as did Millie, but she stuck to her guns. She genuinely couldn't face more questions from Julia. There was so much she couldn't tell her; couldn't tell anyone. Julia would only despise her. Lord knew, she'd certainly despised herself at times. She'd known only too well what she should do. She just hadn't been able to muster up the will, or the courage, to do it. Until that final day, when she'd accepted she had to leave …

*   *   *

With Millie still grumbling, she unlocked the front door of Primrose Cottage and they went inside.

'Mummy,' Millie said as she hopped around, legs crossed tightly, 'I want the loo.'

'Okay, come on then. Upstairs.'

There wasn't a downstairs toilet, which was a bit of a nuisance with a three-year-old. The little girl charged up and ran into the bathroom.

'Mummy,' she wailed, 'I've wet my knickers.'

'Oh, Millie. Why didn't you say something at Auntie Julia's? You could have gone there.'

'I didn't want to then.' Millie sounded cross, as if Tory was being incredibly stupid.

'Okay.' She pulled the wet knickers off and lifted the little girl onto the toilet. 'I'll go and get you a clean pair.' She turned to leave the bathroom, and it was then that she noticed it. The towels on the rail were perfectly and symmetrically arranged. This time she knew she hadn't left them like that. She hated that formal look. It always reminded her of hotel bathrooms. She preferred them more loosely arranged. In other words, untidy.

'Millie,' she said softly, 'did you straighten the towels?'

'No, Mummy. You must have done it.'

Tory frowned, uncertainty gripping her once again. Had she? If she had, she couldn't for the life of her recall doing it. It had been the same with the cans in the kitchen cupboard. For the second time, she asked herself if the habit of keeping things in perfect order had become so ingrained in her that she was doing it instinctively. But why now? Why not when they'd first arrived here?

4

Tory's anxiety eased as the evening wore on. As she repeatedly assured herself, no one knew she was here. The only person she had told was her mother, Janey. She'd been feeling increasingly guilty at not having been in touch, so she'd rung her a couple of months after arriving in Compton Cross. But even then, she'd only revealed the name of the village — no road name, no house number. And that had been on the condition that Janey told no one else at all.

'Well, all right,' Janey had reluctantly agreed, 'but I just don't understand why you've done all this. You simply upped and disappeared. You haven't been in touch. We've all been frantic with worry. Stuart, especially. Why would you leave such a good husband? You couldn't have wished for a better man. Surely you could telephone him? Why are you being so cruel? I simply don't understand. He's given you everything.'

'I'm sorry, Mum.'

'I've tried ringing your mobile phone several times, but couldn't get through.'

'No, you wouldn't. I've bought a new one, a pay-as-you-go, with a different number. I'm sorry.' Did she have to keep saying that? It wasn't her fault she'd had to leave, though clearly her mother thought it was. 'It was something I needed to do. I'll keep in touch, but for now, bye.'

'Wait,' she heard her mother cry, 'give me your new number …'

But Tory didn't want to do that. She didn't want anyone to be able to contact her. She'd felt terrible afterwards about her secrecy, but her mother would never cope with the truth. Tory had tried ringing the house a couple of times since then, but upon her father answering, she'd instantly ended the call. Her mother had always refused to have a mobile phone, so that wasn't an option. She'd even rung the fashion store where her mother worked as manager, but no one had answered. Which wasn't unusual. If they were busy, they tended to ignore the ringing of the phone.

As for her father and Bella, her sister, she'd never been close to either of them. Bella was ten years younger, so they'd never really done much together. And her father was ... well, he was a lazy bully.

Anyway, she was here now, and here she was going to stay. But — and no matter how she tried, she couldn't dismiss the notion — supposing her mother had let slip the name Compton Cross?

*   *   *

Monday morning, as it invariably did, came round all too soon. Tory dropped Millie off at Julia's and walked on to work. The sunshine that they'd enjoyed for the past couple of days had disappeared, and the morning was a miserably cold one with the sky a leaden grey that threatened snow. Even as she had the thought, a few flakes began to fall. She smiled. Millie would be thrilled. She'd hardly ever seen snow.

But as the day progressed, the prospect didn't seem quite so appealing. More and more fell, and by the time she left the shop late that afternoon several inches were lying on the pavement. She grimaced down at her completely unsuitable footwear. Her shoes were flat-soled, it was true, but even so, they offered little or no protection from either the cold or the snow. And their grip wasn't great, either.

Having little choice in the matter, however, she set off, slithering and sliding with every step she took. A couple of times she lost her balance and almost fell. How on earth was she going to get Millie home in this? She frowned. She should have listened to a weather forecast that morning. Why hadn't she? God, she could be so stupid at times. She peered upwards, squinting against the fast-falling snow. At this rate she wasn't even going to get to Julia's, let alone back to the cottage. She groaned.

Huge flakes were now falling so thickly

that she could barely see ahead, and the wind was picking up. Tory started to feel a sense of real panic — at the exact moment that her feet slid from beneath her and, once again, she felt herself going down. Just like last time, there was nothing she could do to save herself. Fortunately, the snow was deep enough to cushion her landing, but even so, she lay for a couple of moments, well and truly winded by the impact.

She heard the purr of a large engine as a vehicle came to a halt alongside her. She lifted her head and squinted through the blizzard-like conditions. It was a black Range Rover. She gave a despairing groan and allowed her head to drop back onto the snow. Of all the cars to come along, it had to be his. Damien Grey's. What the hell was he going to say when he saw her, flat on her back for a second time? Something derisive, no doubt, if his last performance was anything to go by. The man was like a bad penny. He just kept turning up, and always at the worst possible time.

She heard the car door open, then the crunching of feet through the snow, and there he was, looming over her. She braced herself for the expected pithy words, and he didn't disappoint her.

'You do seem to make a habit of falling down,' he smoothly said. 'Is it the mere sight of me? I must say, I've never had quite such a dramatic effect before.' He couldn't hide his utterly predictable amusement as he asked, 'Are you okay? Give me your hand. I'm getting quite practised in rescuing you from difficult situations.'

She didn't bother responding to that. She simply did as he asked, and proffered her hand. He hauled her to her feet before bending over and brushing the snow from her.

'Thank you,' she muttered. 'I wasn't expecting all this snow, or I would have worn some boots.'

'Don't you listen to the local weather forecast before setting out in the mornings? It would be good idea at this time of the year. They were quite confident in predicting this.'

'I didn't have the radio on — I was far too busy getting both Millie and myself ready to go out.'

'Well, I'm sure you'll take care to listen in the future,' he smoothly said. 'Now, I think I'd better give you a lift. You won't get very far in those.' He stared down at her shoes.

'I have to collect Millie from my friend Julia's house. She looks after Millie while I go to work,' she said.

'Fine. Direct me there and we'll fetch her.'

'But you don't have a child seat.'

'Does your friend have one we could borrow?'

Mutely, Tory nodded.

'Great. I'll drop it straight back round to her once I've got you and your daughter home.'

Tory wearily closed her eyes. Julia would have a field day when Tory turned up accompanied by the notorious Damien Grey. She could already hear Julia's 'Won't you introduce me?'. She'd then flutter her eyelids and give a seductive smile, as she held out her dainty and immaculately manicured hand. Tory gave a silent groan as she imagined the conversation. 'We haven't met,' Julia would go on. 'I'd certainly remember if we had.' There would then be an even more seductive smile. Yet again, it was all so predictable. Not least because she'd seen Julia in action before. Tory sighed.

Even so, she wasn't mad enough to turn down the offer of a lift, not in these conditions. The snow was deepening with every moment that passed. She allowed herself to be assisted to the front passenger door and then virtually lifted into the seat. She felt extremely foolish and incredibly stupid — and not for the first time, as far as Damien Grey was concerned. However, displaying an unexpected and totally uncharacteristic restraint, he made no comment. Instead, he gingerly picked his way round to the driver's side and climbed in. It seemed his shoes weren't any more snow-worthy than hers. She permitted herself a smug smile.

'Okay,' he said with a slanting glance, 'where to?'

'Wheeler Street, number eighteen.'

'I know it.'

She stared at him in some surprise. 'Do you?' Had Julia been holding out on her? Had Damien visited her at some time?

'Oh, I don't mean I know the house. I mean the street. One of my cleaners lives there.'

Of course she did, Tory mused. *One* of his cleaners? How many did he have, for heaven's sake? Then again, with a house the size of Compton Court he'd probably need a whole platoon of them. She gave a soft snort of derision. He shot a glance at her but, despite clearly having heard her, he didn't say anything. Swiftly she rearranged her features into an expression of calm indifference. Even so, something — vexation? — kindled momentarily in his eyes. She'd better watch out. She was quite sure that if she upset him enough he'd have no compunction about turfing her out of his car.

They set off slowly, the wheels spinning as they fought for a grip on the snow-covered road. Tory swallowed nervously. There must be conditions, surely, that even a Range Rover wouldn't be able to cope with? Supposing they got stuck? The mere notion of being trapped in the limited confines of this vehicle, as roomy as it was, with this man, was an intimidating one. She glanced through the side window. There was hardly a soul about, everyone evidently having taken sensible precautions and headed for home as early and as quickly as they could.

He gave her a sideways glance. 'How was your day?'

'Unusually busy for a Monday.'

'The more sensible people stocking up before the bad week to come, presumably.'

Was that more criticism of her lack of forethought? If it was, he gave no indication of it, so reluctantly she gave him the benefit of the doubt. 'Probably.'

He swung off the main street and headed along Wheeler Street.

'It's about halfway along,' she told him, 'on the left.'

The lights were all on at Julia's, and Julia was standing in the front window, anxiously peering out — looking for Tory, no doubt. Her eyes widened and her mouth dropped open as she took in the sight of the large black car pulling up in front of her driveway. She disappeared, only to reappear almost at once at the front door. Millie was at her side, coat and hat already on.

'Mummy, Mummy,' she cried as Tory climbed from the vehicle and began to gingerly negotiate her way across the pavement and then the short distance to the house.

'Hi, sweetheart,' she called back, ignoring Julia's broad grin as she took in the sight of the man with her friend.

'What's this, then?' she soundlessly mouthed as she smoothed her honey -blonde bob, ensuring that every strand of hair was exactly where it should be. Next she swiftly set about straightening her sweater, before tightening the belt around her waist to emphasise its slimness.

In the aftermath of all this activity, Tory didn't need to look to know that Damien was right behind her. She'd been praying he'd stay in the car. Having no other option, she introduced him — although she suspected that Julia knew full well who he was.

'This is Mr Grey. Damien Grey.' She followed this up with, 'Mr Grey, meet my friend, Julia. Mr Grey has very kindly offered Millie and me a lift home. Julia, I don't suppose we could borrow Millie's car seat?'

At the sight of her friend's eyelashes beginning to flutter — as she'd known they would — she gritted her teeth and waited for the pantomime to begin. It didn't take long.

'Yes, of course,' said Julia, picking up her car keys from the hall table and pressing the unlock button, before turning her attention once more to Damien. 'And hello, Mr Grey,' she breathily said. 'I think I've seen you round the village once or twice.'

'Pleased to meet you, Julia. The truth is, I couldn't bring myself to leave your friend lying at my feet — again.' He grinned broadly. 'It's the second time in a week I've had to pick her up.' He glanced at the tight-lipped Tory and went on, 'Do you think she's trying to tell me something?'

'Well,' Julia purred, 'if it were me, I surely would be.' She smiled, lowering her lashes now over a pair of dark blue eyes that were gleaming with lust. 'Why don't the two of you come in for a drink? You must need one after all your excitement.'

'Oh no,' Tory hastened to say. She didn't know how much more of this flirting she could take. 'I need to get Millie home, and I'm sure Mr Grey has things he wants to do.'

'Not really,' Damien murmured, returning Julia's unspoken come-on with a look of his own. 'My evening's my own. And it's Damien. Much more friendly than Mr Grey, don't you think?'

'I do,' Julia agreed, bestowing another warm look upon him.

Tory stoically ignored all that was

passing between her friend and Damien, though she did allow herself a muted snort. He hadn't invited her to call him Damien. Typical. Thoroughly irritated by now, especially by the antics of her best friend, she said, 'Come along, darling,' and she held out her hand out to Millie.

'All right, sweetheart,' Damien teasingly responded, a mischievous gleam lighting his eye.

'I wasn't talking to you,' Tory stiffly told him.

'Shame. I thought it was my lucky day.' And to Tory's vexation, he winked at Julia, before pulling a face of wildly exaggerated disappointment. 'After all, it's not that often that I'm in the company of two such lovely women.'

Julia tittered. 'Ooh, thank you. Ignore Tory.' She waved her fingers dismissively at her friend before theatrically whispering to Damien, 'She's often in a bad humour at the end of the day.'

Tory wanted to scream at them both. They were making fun of her, and she'd thought better of Julia. She glared at her friend, but Julia seemed impervious. Mainly because her gaze was riveted on Damien. Tory took hold of Millie's hand and literally yanked her towards Julia's car.

'Mummy, you're hurting me!'

'Sorry, sweetie,' she murmured, whilst going through the rigmarole of unlatching Millie's car seat and hefting it out.

She glanced backwards then at the other two, only to find Damien watching her from beneath lowered lids, his expression veiled and inscrutable. She heard Julia say, in the throaty tones that she used whenever she encountered an attractive man, 'It's been an absolute delight to meet you, Damien. Maybe we can have that drink another time? Tory,' she then called, 'I'll see you in the morning.'

Tory would have loved to say, 'No, you won't.' But, of course, she couldn't. Instead she said, 'Fine, providing we're not snowed in.'

She and Millie had reached his Damien's, which was still unlocked. Tory wrestled the car seat into the back and secured it.

'Go ahead,' he said from just behind her, 'hop in.' He then lifted Millie onto the seat and belted her in. She smiled up at him, her dimples on full display, every bit as charmed as Julia had been.

Tory simply gritted her teeth and started to climb in too. However, as she did so her feet began to slide from under her, the passenger door being next to a particularly treacherous stretch of pavement. Instinctively, she made a grab for Damien. He didn't hesitate. He slid an arm around her waist and clamped her to him. She stared up at him. Their mouths were only an inch apart. His breath feathered the skin of her face as the scent of his aftershave filled her nostrils, making her head spin dizzily as the heat of desire swamped her. She gasped and pulled away from him.

'Really, have you no shame, woman?' Julia called. 'Falling into a virtual stranger's arms?' And she laughed uproariously.

'Oh, shut up,' Tory muttered. Damien was laughing too, she noticed. All of a sudden she felt completely excluded from their merriment. It was humiliating. What was wrong with them both? They were behaving like silly children. Crossly, she looked back at her friend. Julia beamed and waved enthusiastically. She clearly didn't see she'd done anything wrong. And why would she? Tory belatedly asked herself. She was a free woman, and Damien was a free man. So why did she feel so miffed? Because she herself wasn't free?

'Mummy,' Millie said from behind her, 'can we build a snowman when we get home?'

'Not tonight, sweetheart,' Tory absently replied.

'Why not?' the little girl wailed.

'Spoilsport,' Damien murmured at her side.

She glared at him, daring him to say anything more. 'It's far too cold,' she explained, 'and it's dark, and still snowing. Maybe tomorrow.' She looked at Millie. The little girl was on the verge of tears. Her heart melted with love. 'I promise. It will have stopped by then, I'm sure.'

But Millie had other tactics in mind. She turned her dewy-eyed gaze towards Damien. He grinned at her via the interior mirror. 'Would you like to build a snowman with me, Damien?'

'Do you know, I would, Millie. It's been far too many years since I've done that.'

Tory stared at him. He was deliberately undermining her. The damned cheek of the man!

'Mummy, Damien will help me. You can stay inside and keep warm.'

'Not tonight, Millie,' he said. 'Your mummy's right. It's too dark and too cold tonight. But I will definitely join you on another occasion.'

'Tomorrow?'

'Tomorrow might be difficult. I have another engagement I really must keep.'

No need to ask who with, Tory thought. Having learnt of his dubious reputation from Julia, it would doubtless be with one of his many women.

'But,' he went on, 'if the snow's still here at the weekend, I'm your man.' He pulled away from the kerbside. 'Chester Road, number twenty-two, right?'

'Yes. It's called Primrose Cottage,' she told him. She was amazed he'd remembered her address so accurately. 'Carry on down this road and it's the third turn on the right. But then, you probably know it,' she finished with more than a hint of irony. One of his cleaners most likely lived along there too. He didn't respond, however.

'All right, the weekend,' Millie's voice came from the rear. 'My daddy probably would have helped me, but I don't see him anymore.'

Damien cast a quick glance at Tory but didn't say anything. Tory remained silent too.

'As soon as I can, I'll help you. I promise,' he reassured a dejected Millie.

To Tory's relief, they'd reached her cottage. It effectively precluded any further conversation or questions from the man at her side. Because, judging by his expression, there were several things he was itching to ask her.

He got out immediately and moved round to Tory's door to help her out. No matter how deeply he irritated her, she couldn't fault his manners — and irrationally, that vexed her too. The snow was deeper here, maybe because it was a quieter road than Julia's, with less traffic. And it was still snowing.

Damien lifted Millie out. The little girl put her arms around his neck and nestled her face into him. She then whispered, raising her wide blue eyes to his, 'Will you come and see me?'

He laughed softly. 'This girl has a bright future, probably on the stage. Of course I will, sweetheart. That's another promise.' He looked at Tory then, offered her an arm and said, 'Let's get you both inside.' He was still holding Millie in his other arm.

'You've completely charmed my daughter,' she coolly told him. Although she felt his gaze upon her, she kept her face turned away.

'And how about her mother? Have I charmed her too?' he quietly asked.

'Well,' she snorted, 'you've certainly charmed Julia.'

He didn't say anything to that. She glanced up at him. His gaze was a hooded one, but even so, she could detect the gleam in his eye. But what that signified, she had no idea. 'Well, I don't know about charmed,' she relented. 'I'm certainly grateful to you. I don't know how Millie and I would have got home tonight without your help.'

His gaze narrowed even further, although the gleam remained. 'That's a start, I suppose,' he drily said.

She immediately felt ungracious; guilty, even. He hadn't had to bring them home. He could have left her to struggle through the deepening snow. Instead, he'd gone out of his way to help her. She softened. 'Well, maybe if you work at it ...' And she couldn't help herself; she grinned at him.

'Oh, believe me,' he throatily declared, 'I fully intend to.'

5

Once Damien had left, Tory undressed Millie and then gave her supper before putting her to bed, and all the while she mulled over Damien's final remarks. He was a highly attractive man. In fact, he was the most handsome man she'd ever encountered. It would be all too easy to fall for him. But the truth was, she didn't feel she could trust him. She didn't feel she could trust any man, come to that; not anymore. They all started out as charming, generous, prepared to do anything for the woman they loved, but then life and its day-to-day practicalities and problems took over, and the romance and the charm began to disintegrate, before finally vanishing altogether.

Sighing heavily, Tory poured herself a large glass of wine, lit the fire, and then sat in an armchair, preparing herself for the memories to flood back. It was time to face up to what had happened; to stop letting it colour and influence her life. To lay the blame where it should be — with Stuart, despite his efforts to make her responsible for it all. She needed to put it behind her, relegate it to the past, even if a divorce was most likely out of the question for the time being.

It had all begun eight years ago. She'd met Stuart at a friend's birthday party. In fact, she learnt later that her friend Sally had been matchmaking. Stuart had been thirty-two to her nineteen at the time, and she'd been completely captivated by him. She could still see his sharply defined cheekbones, his firm jawline, the intense blue of his eyes — eyes that were filled with admiration for her, and then, pretty quickly, with love. He hadn't been a tall man — five feet ten inches, with a slender build. He'd been immaculately dressed in an open-necked blue shirt the exact colour of his eyes, and tailored dark trousers. He'd exuded self-confidence and intelligence. He talked with great knowledge about many things. He was, unarguably, a man of the world. He told her all about his travels to Europe, Russia, the USA, Africa — she'd been completely dazzled by him. Then he'd told her he was a partner in a reputable and very well-known accountancy firm; that he had his own house, and a Jaguar — it all combined to overwhelm her; overawe her, even. She'd repeatedly asked herself why a man like that was so interested in her.

But, unbelievably, he had been, and they'd spent the entire evening together — dancing, laughing, talking. They'd seemed made for each other. He was all she'd ever wanted in a man. From then on they met every evening, and spent every Saturday and Sunday in each other's company. Friends jokingly asked if they were actually attached at the hip.

Stuart didn't rush her in any way, but he also made no secret of his passionate desire for her. He complimented her; flattered her. It had only been a matter of weeks before she was head-over-heels in love. So when, just three months on, he asked her to marry him, she had no hesitation in agreeing. She moved in with him mere days later, both of them too impatient to wait for the actual wedding ceremony that would make them man and wife. Six months afterwards, they were married.

He seemed to be the husband every girl dreams of. As well as being a passionate lover, he was a generous man. He frequently bought her presents — a single red rose laid alongside her breakfast plate, half a dozen Belgian handmade chocolates artistically arranged on her pillow at night, a book she'd been wanting, a DVD. Their tastes matched completely. They were totally compatible. 'A match made in heaven,' he was fond of telling their friends.

Their wedding day had been like something from a fairytale, with a snowy white gown for Tory and a veil that trailed behind her by a full five feet — Tory hadn't wanted this, but Stuart had insisted. 'I want you to look like the princess you are, my darling.' There were three bridesmaids, all dressed in the exact blue of Stuart's eyes; he'd insisted on this, too. She'd thought several years later that this almost obsessive need should have been some sort of warning to her. He'd thrown a sumptuous banquet afterwards and they'd enjoyed an expensive honeymoon in Barbados. Stuart had insisted on paying for everything. 'Whatever you want, my love, you shall have.' But really, it had been whatever Stuart wanted. Tory hadn't had much say in any of it. She hadn't minded at the time. If Stuart was happy, she was happy. Her father, of course, willingly — eagerly, even — had handed over all financial responsibility to his future son-in-law.

'You're a very lucky girl, Victoria,' her mother repeatedly told her. Her father just grumbled, 'Waste of money.'

'Well, seeing as it's not your money,' Tory had muttered, 'why are you moaning?'

He'd heard her and raised a threatening hand. She'd backed off. It wouldn't have been the first time he'd struck her. He was a bully, dominating both her mother and herself. He was also bone-idle. He hadn't worked in ten years. 'Bad back. It's excruciatingly painful,' he'd tell everyone. 'I hate being at home, but ... And at least Janey's out earning. My disability pension wouldn't go far.'

No, Tory would think, *especially when it all goes on your beer and cigarettes.*

The only one of them he seemed to love was Bella; he doted on her, always finding a few pounds in his back pocket to give her.

'Well, Victoria's mum's favourite,' she would tell people — they'd all called her Victoria — 'so it's only fair I'm Dad's.'

Tory always thought that Bella had a girlish-crush on Stuart. Both she and Janey adored him. He could do no wrong in their eyes.

Their first couple of years of married life were blissfully happy, and Tory hadn't been able to believe her luck in finding and holding on to someone like him. But gradually, almost unnoticeably, he began to criticise her, gently and fondly to begin with. 'Darling, you left wet towels all over the bathroom floor this morning. I've picked them up for you.' And then he'd give a rueful smile, as if it weren't really that important.

'Oh, did I?' she'd say. 'I was in a bit of a rush. Sorry, darling, I'll try to do better from now on.'

'If you would,' he'd reply, and that was that.

And she did try — after all, it took only seconds to re-hang towels on the rail. But then he began tidying the kitchen cupboards, again after gently complaining that nothing was in the right order. He'd regularly spend his first half hour or so at home in the evening rearranging cans and jars, packets of food, cups and saucers, plates and glasses, grouping things together in neat rows and stacks.

'Stuart,' she laughed one day, 'does it really matter if the baked beans aren't all together and in regimented rows?'

He'd turned on her, his eyes dark, almost black, flashing with anger. 'Yes, it does. I don't want to have to spend several minutes each day searching for things

I want. I like to know exactly where they are. And, frankly, I've got better things to do with my time.'

Then it was the cutlery drawer. She'd mixed up the spoons and forks. He loudly clattered them as he replaced them in their proper sections. Again, she'd chuckled.

'I hadn't realised what a tidy person you are …'

He'd swung round, raised his hand, and slapped her across the face. 'Don't you ever laugh at me.'

Shocked, Tory had lifted her hand to her tingling cheek. 'Stuart!' she'd gasped.

'Oh, my God.' He'd instantly looked as shocked as she felt. His face had drained of colour and his mouth had trembled. 'My love, I'm so sorry. I didn't mean to do that. Please, forgive me.' He'd pulled her into his arms, tears filling his eyes. 'Please.' His cheeks had been wet as he cradled her, kissing her burning face, caressing her. 'Victoria, I love you so much. I didn't mean that. Really, I didn't.' And they'd ended up making love on the kitchen floor.

Tory had told herself later that it had been a silly one-off incident and it would never happen again. She'd play her part. She'd learn to be tidy, to do the things he wanted her to. And as the following months passed happily, she gradually forgot all about it. Until one evening, she was late back from work. Stuart was waiting for her.

She walked into the kitchen calling, 'I'm home, love.'

He was standing motionless, his hips propped against the worktop, his arms crossed in front of him. 'So I see,' he sneered. He then looked pointedly up at the wall clock. 'Would you care to tell me just where you've been? Who you've been with?' His voice was icy, controlled. His eyes were dark with contempt and suspicion.

'I've been at work,' she stammered. 'Where else would I have been?'

'Who else was there?'

'No one. I was on my own.' Her voice shook. 'There were some letters I had to get into the post tonight. The clients have been waiting for them.'

'I don't believe you.' He strode towards her, thrusting his face forward until they were practically nose to nose. She instinctively backed away from him. His expression darkened as his mouth compressed into a thin line. 'What's wrong? Are you scared you smell of him? Of sex? Tell me the truth. Which one of your bosses are you screwing? David Harper? Bill Smith? They're both about your age, aren't they? Give or take a couple of years.'

'Stuart, please — there's nothing like that. They're both happily married.'

'Since when has that stopped anyone? And you? Are you ready for a bit of younger flesh, eh? Maybe a man my age isn't enough for you?'

'No,' she cried. 'I love you — I don't want anyone else.'

His blue eyes were almost black now as he stared at her, such was his fury. 'Look at you.' He flicked his hand at her. 'Dressed like a tart.' His top lip curled. 'With your short skirt, your tight blouse.

Don't forget, I know how easy you can be. It didn't take me long to get you into bed, did it?'

She gasped, as tears filled her eyes and overflowed down her face.

'Oh there she goes, snivelling. The last resort of all women. Such frail little creatures. Can't take any sort of criticism. Well, it won't wash with me.' He grabbed hold of her by the shoulders and began to shake her, back and forth, her head rocking agonisingly.

'Please, Stuart. My head ...'

He snorted. 'Oh, and now she's got a headache. I bet you didn't say that to your lover.' He gave another, even harder, shake. 'I don't want to come home to an empty house. You know how hard I work.' He shook her again — just once — and then pushed her violently away from him.

She stumbled backwards, lost her balance and fell, her head striking the edge of the granite worktop as she went down.

'Stuart — don't,' she cried, lifting her hands to her face as he moved towards her and bent over her, his one arm raised. 'Please, don't hit me.'

He stopped and stared down at her as she cowered away from him on the floor. He regarded her, his expression changing from fury into one of despair.

'Victoria,' he moaned, 'why do you make me do these things? Why?'

'I don't.' She slid backwards on her bottom, moving as far away from him as she could, until her back was pressed flat against a cupboard door and she could retreat no further. But her contradiction, as low and as soft as it was, only reactivated his anger.

'Yes,' he shouted, 'you do.' His eyes narrowed at her, full of menace. He leant right down towards her, almost bending double, so that his face was only an inch from hers. She could feel his hot breath upon her skin. She tried not to flinch away from him, knowing it would only anger him even more. 'You deliberately provoke me, Victoria. Normally I ignore it, but today I'm tired; stressed. I've had a hell of a day.'

And suddenly, all his rage seemed to desert him and he slumped down onto the floor, raising both hands to his face as he began to cry deep, racking sobs as his shoulders heaved and his whole body shook. 'Oh God,' he moaned.

Tory sat quite still for a long, long moment, scared, not knowing what to do. But then she slid slowly towards him. 'Stuart, please don't.'

He reached out for her. Despite making every effort not to, she flinched away. He wept even harder.

'Stuart, darling — please don't. It's all right, really.' She wrapped her arms about him then, rocking him as if he were a child, crooning, 'Ssh, it's okay; it's all okay.'

'Victoria, I'm sorry. I don't want to do these things, but …'

'Come on, let's get up and I'll get us a drink. We'll talk it through. I'm sure we can work it out.'

So that's what they did. Once again, Tory convinced herself it was a one-off incident. Stuart was such a charming man; this wasn't typical of him. He must be extremely stressed at work, she decided. She'd have to learn not to upset him. It was her fault. She was so thoughtless, so careless, so untidy. She'd have to make sure she left things exactly as he liked them. He was so proud of his home. He'd done so much to improve it. It was only natural he'd want it to remain perfect.

But no matter what she told herself, from that day on things got progressively worse. He'd rant and lash out at the slightest thing. She'd actually reached the point of considering leaving him when she discovered she was pregnant. They'd never taken any precautions — foolishly, she'd belatedly conceded. But they'd both wanted a family, Stuart even more than she did. Probably because he was thirteen years older than her and felt they should get on with it before he was too old. And after four and a half years of failing to conceive, she hadn't given any thought to contraception; in fact, she'd begun to believe she was infertile.

At first, looking at the positive test, she'd felt only despair, but then hope reared its head. Maybe this was what they needed; what he needed? A new life to protect? To take care of. And he did seem genuinely thrilled when she told him her news.

'Oh, my darling. What a clever girl you are. Now, we must look after you. You'll give up work of course.'

'Oh, but I …' She hadn't for a single second thought he'd expect that. She'd planned to go on working until the last moment.

'No, Victoria, I insist. We can't take any chances with this precious baby. We'll be a real family.'

And her life did improve from that time on, markedly. He looked after her; virtually waited on her when he was at home. If, occasionally, things weren't exactly as he wanted, he'd moan, even rant at times, but he never once raised a hand to her. Perhaps this would prove to be their turning point? Their salvation? Perhaps they could recapture the happiness of their early years of marriage? As parents, that was what they both must want, surely? A happy family unit.

And that was what seemed set to happen. He started buying her presents again, something he hadn't done for quite a while. He cooked for her; cherished her. And when Millie was born, with his blue eyes and dark hair, Stuart became a devoted father. Nothing was too good for his little girl. He spent hours playing with her. He proudly showed her off to anyone who displayed the slightest interest. He carried a small photo album in his briefcase and pulled it out at the first opportunity. Gradually, Tory relaxed. The worst was over, she told herself. Things could only get better.

And they did, until Millie was two years old. Then gradually, almost imperceptibly to begin with, he reverted to type. He never, ever struck Tory in front of Millie, and he was very careful to only hit her where the bruises he left wouldn't show, but hit her he did. Frequently, and hard. He also began to expect sex on demand, and if she refused because Millie was there with them, he'd take the little girl upstairs, place her in her cot, close her bedroom door, and return to force himself upon Tory. It didn't matter where they were; he wouldn't take no for an answer. 'You are my wife and you will behave like a wife. When I want you, you'll be there — ready and willing. Is that clear?'

Then one day, when Millie was approaching her third birthday, Tory heard him shouting at her. Millie cried out, 'No, Daddy!' They were in Millie's room.

Tory practically flew up the stairs, taking them two at a time. She erupted into her daughter's room to see Stuart standing over her, his hand raised ready to slap her. Tory leapt between them.

'Don't you dare,' she hissed. 'Don't you touch her.'

Stuart regarded her, his mouth compressed, his eyes two dark pebbles, a sure indication that he was about to lose his temper completely. 'She knows she should tidy her toys away every evening and she's refusing. She's old enough now to understand that. She has to learn,

Victoria, just like you have.' His tone was steely; detached. It was as if he were somewhere else entirely; remote, removed physically from her and Millie.

Tory lifted her crying daughter into her arms. 'We'll do it together, baby, won't we?'

'Yes, Mummy,' Millie hiccupped. She then sobbed, 'Is Daddy going to smack me?'

'No, of course he isn't. Daddy will go downstairs and we'll put everything away.'

It was at that moment she knew she couldn't stay. She and Millie had to leave; go somewhere where he couldn't find them. Run away and hide, in other words. She wasn't taking any chances with her daughter's well-being.

The next morning, once Stuart had departed for work, Tory calmly and methodically packed everything she had room in the car for, strapped Millie into her car seat, and drove away. But first of all, she paid a visit to the bank and drew out every penny she had. It wasn't a lot, but it would last them a month or two if she was frugal. At least until she found herself a job.

As she left Warwickshire behind, she realised she had no idea where she was going. She had told no one of her intention, not even her mother. She couldn't rely on her not to tell Stuart. And somehow, completely by chance, she ended up in Compton Cross and overnight became Tory, not Victoria.

But even though she'd found them a house so that they had somewhere to live, she remained deeply troubled; nervous. For the first two months, she anxiously scanned a daily newspaper and watched all the television news broadcasts she could, terrified that Stuart would have reported them missing and begun a nationwide police search.

But gradually, when nothing happened; when neither her nor Millie's names were mentioned as missing persons, she relaxed. He hadn't told the police. She guessed that he was afraid that if Tory was found she'd tell the world of his mistreatment of her, and that she had increasingly feared for her daughter's safety.

As the weeks passed and no one came looking for her, she began to believe that she'd got away with it. He must have persuaded her mother not to go to the police as well, but she guessed that wouldn't have been difficult. She'd have believed everything he told her; she'd adored him every bit as much as Bella had.

She knew what he'd say. She could hear him as clearly as if he were there with her: 'Mark my words, Janey — she'll be back. There's no need to involve the police. She left of her own volition, after all, taking luggage for her and Millie. She won't survive on her own for long. Not without me. Don't worry.'

But now she wondered whether Stuart had indeed found them. Everything was beginning to point that way. And if that were the case, then someone had told him where she was; they must have. Otherwise, why would he have shown up here, in a backwater village in the middle of nowhere? And looked at logically, if the snooper was him, it could only have been her mother who had said something.

Tory's feeling of betrayal was immense. Her mother obviously blamed Tory for the breakup of the marriage. Stuart would have spun her some tale, placing all the blame on Tory, and she would have believed him. Maybe it was time to ring her again and tell her the truth of what had happened; find out whether it was possible that Stuart did indeed know where she and Millie were? And more importantly, was he still at their house in Warwickshire? Because if he wasn't, then it was highly probable he'd found her. And what then?

Her heart sank. She couldn't face running away again. She'd made friends here, and Millie was happy. The last thing she wanted was to leave. So what the hell was she going to do?

6

To think had always been to act as far as Tory was concerned, so she tapped out the number on her mobile phone and hoped it would be her mother who answered. It was a good time to make the call; her father would be in the pub, and Bella, she was confident, would also be out. From the age of fourteen, she'd invariably gone out in the evenings to meet her friends.

This time, Tory's luck was in. 'Hello?'

'Mum, it's me.'

'Victoria! Thank goodness. I've been waiting to hear from you. It's been so long. If you'd told me your new number, I could have rung you.' The criticism — accusation, even — was unmissable.

'I did try and contact you a couple of times, but you weren't there. I'm sorry, Mum.' And she genuinely was. It hadn't been easy to remain distant from Janey.

They'd been so close.

'I've been almost out of my mind. How could you have done this to us all? Just disappearing — and taking Millie, too? It's heartless. I thought better of you, I really did.'

'I told you last time we spoke, Mum. I had to do it.'

'Why? Why did you have to do it? It was so selfish, so — cruel.'

Tory cut in. 'I couldn't take any more, Mum.' And she went on to describe, slowly and in detail, all that Stuart had done to her, before concluding with, 'When he threatened to hit Millie, well, I knew we had to go.'

'I can't believe it,' Janey said, audibly shocked. 'Not of Stuart. He's always been a wonderful man; a wonderful father. He loves you both so much.'

'Mum,' Tory cried, 'please believe me. He hit me, again and again. I had bruises under my clothes which you never saw; nobody did. I put up with it for years.' Her voice broke. 'I couldn't have him treating Millie the same way. Surely you

94

can see that?'

Her mother fell silent. Then, 'You should have told me, Victoria.' Her voice broke too.

'I couldn't, Mum. I was too ashamed to admit what was happening, even to you. He convinced me it was all my fault. He'd tell me that if I'd just do things properly he wouldn't have to hit me. And after we left, I didn't want him to have any way of tracing us.' Tory began to quietly cry. 'So I told no one where we were, other than you. And I kept that to the bare minimum. It wasn't what I wanted, Mum, but it seemed the only way to keep us safe.'

'Oh, my darling. I'm so sorry.' Janey fell silent again. 'Victoria,' she whispered, 'he knows where you are — the name of the village, anyway.'

'How? Oh, Mum, you didn't tell him?'

Janey paused before answering. 'I didn't tell Stuart.'

'Who did you tell then?' Tory demanded.

'Your dad had been going on and on

about you running off and taking his only grandchild, and in the end he wore me down, and I told him — Compton Cross. But I said that he mustn't on any account tell anyone else. You were so adamant you wanted it kept secret. That was all, I promise. But apparently Bella overheard me, and thinking she was helping him, she went straight to Stuart and told him. He went absolutely crazy, apparently, ranting and raving about you and how he'd make you pay — I think he frightened her. Enough to confess to me what she'd done. I'm so sorry. It's my fault. I wanted to ring and tell you, but with no number ...'

Tory's heart went into freefall. 'He's here then. It all adds up. There's been some man snooping around the village, peering into windows. Stuart, trying to locate us, presumably.'

'Oh, God. I'm so sorry.'

'How long has he been gone?'

'A couple of weeks, maybe three. I'm not absolutely sure when he went.'

'He's found us then.' Her voice broke

into a small sob.

'Oh, darling, I'm so sorry.'

'Millie said she saw someone in the garden late one night. He's been wearing some sort of disguise — a hat pulled right down over his face, so she didn't recognise him. He saw her looking out of her window and waved to her. I'd left my car on the drive that night instead of putting it into the garage as I usually do, so he would have recognised it. How could I have been so stupid?' She began to quietly weep. Then, angry with herself for her weakness, she dashed her tears away.

But there was something she didn't understand. If he knew where they were, why didn't he come to the cottage and talk to her face to face, instead of just rearranging things in the house? It didn't make sense. Or — she shivered — did it? Was this his way of frightening her? Punishing her, as he would see it, for leaving him? It was exactly the sort of thing he'd do. And he'd told Bella he'd make her pay. Her heart raced with a sickening ferocity. What would he be capable of doing, now that she'd left him of her own free will? He'd see that as an utterly humiliating rejection of him, and for that he'd never forgive her. Which meant that she and Millie were in danger.

'It doesn't sound like Stuart, Victoria. Sneaking around.' But Janey didn't sound entirely convinced about that.

'It is him, I'm positive. And what's more, he's been into the cottage. Things have been moved, rearranged and placed precisely in order, just like he used to do. He wants me to know he's here.'

'My God, Victoria! Is he really that devious, that cunning?'

'Yes, he is.'

And yet, she couldn't help wondering why she hadn't spotted him. It was only a small village, after all. Though there were several hotels round and about that he could stay in anonymously. If he only travelled into Compton Cross after dark, she would perhaps be unlikely to see him.

'Do you want me to come and stay with you?' her mother asked.

'No, no, Mum. I'll handle it. Don't worry.' Huh! She sounded so positive. If only she felt that way. 'Now,' she went on, 'you'd better have my new mobile number — but please, Mum, don't give it to anyone else. I don't want Stuart getting hold of it and ringing me. And please only ring me in an emergency.' The last thing she wanted was for her number to appear on any list of calls made to her parents' landline. She wouldn't put it past Stuart to somehow check on that. Though if he'd found her, as she was more and more convinced he had, he'd have no need to.

'I won't, I promise. I'm sorry, Victoria. Ring me if you need me; if you need anything. Are you okay for money?'

'I'm fine. I'm working, so …'

'Well, ring me. I can always get some to you. I don't want you and Millie going without.'

Tory ended the call, feeling a hundred times better now that her mother knew the truth of what had happened. For starters, she didn't feel so alone.

It still didn't help her to sleep that

night, however. When she did eventually drop off, her rest was plagued by dark, disturbing dreams of Stuart peering through her window, eyes dark with fury as he hammered on the glass with his fists and shouted, 'I'm coming for you! And when I get to you, you'll wish you'd never been born!'

*   *   *

It was a relief to leave her bed the next morning, wake Millie, and show her the deep snow outside. More had fallen overnight, blanketing the garden in a thick, glistening mantle. Every bush, every tree was covered, the startling whiteness vividly outlining each branch and twig in an intricate lacework against the periwinkle sky.

Millie clapped her hands in delight. 'Can we build a snowman, Mummy — please?'

'Okay,' she eventually said, not having the heart to refuse her. She eyed the kitchen clock. They had ten minutes to spare. 'Quickly then, get your coat and boots on and we'll do a little one.'

It was swiftly accomplished. A perfect snowman, just two feet high, with one of Millie's older scarves tied round its neck, a carrot for a nose and two marbles for eyes. Millie was thrilled. She crouched before it and flung her arms around its neck.

'Not too tightly, darling. You don't want to knock its head off. We haven't got time to rebuild him.'

As it was one of Millie's nursery days, they needed to get a move on. Tory had to drop her off at Julia's in good time. She debated taking the car, but the snow was so deep, she decided they'd be quicker — and safer — walking.

'Will Mr Snowman still be there tonight when we get home?' Millie asked as they set off along the road towards Julia's. 'We could build a friend for him.'

'We'll have to see. It might be too cold by then.'

She rang Julia's doorbell and kissed Millie on her cheek. The door opened and Julia sang out, 'Hi, there.' She then made a great play of glancing around. 'No Damien this morning then?'

'Of course not,' Tory curtly answered. 'Why did you think he'd be with us?' She still felt miffed at the way Julia and Damien had collaborated, as she saw it, in their teasing of her.

'Well,' Julia said, eyeing her and clearly sensing her mood, 'he looked pretty keen last night. I was quite jealous. Tell you what, though.' Her eyes twinkled wickedly. 'If you don't want him, I'll have a go.'

'Go ahead,' Tory told her. 'He's not my type.'

'Not your type?' Julia hooted. 'Are you kidding me? He's every woman's type.'

Ignoring that, Tory said, 'Goodbye, Julia. I'll see you later. Bye, precious.' She dropped another kiss onto Millie's cheek.

She did wonder, fleetingly, whether she should confide in Julia. It would be comforting to have an ally she could turn to here in the village. And it would be another pair of eyes on the lookout for Stuart. The only drawback was that Julia could be a bit of a blabbermouth at times, and the last thing Tory wanted was for her private business to be trumpeted far and wide. But apart from that, if Stuart was here in the village, and somehow learnt that she'd been badmouthing him — well, who knew how he'd react?

She'd keep it to herself for a while longer, she concluded.

★ ★ ★

But she swiftly revised that decision upon arriving home with Millie after work. Because when the little girl eagerly rushed through the house and out of the back door into the garden, the first thing Tory heard was her loud scream: 'Mummy, Mummy!' The girl began to sob loudly.

Tory rushed out after her. And what she saw there before her had her stomach churning with a sick dread. Chunks of what had been Millie's precious snowman were scattered all round the garden: the scarf torn off and trampled onto the snow; the carrot and marbles lying, neatly arranged, alongside. And between all the pieces were a man's footprints.

7

Tory grabbed hold of her daughter's hand and ran her quickly back inside the house. Millie was weeping as though her little heart was breaking. She'd built her first snowman ever and someone had cruelly smashed it to pieces. Once they were inside, Tory picked her up, kissed her, and said, 'We'll make another one tomorrow.'

'But the snow might be gone by then,' she wailed.

But all Tory could think was that someone had been in the garden, and the only possible access to it was either over a fence that was far too high to climb easily — or through the house.

It was Stuart. Who else could it be? And he was sending her a message: this could be you, broken and hurt.

But how was he getting in? Had he learnt to pick locks? The front door lock?

She wouldn't be surprised. There wasn't much he couldn't learn to do once he put his mind to it. She recalled him deciding to add another bathroom, an en-suite in their bedroom. Rather than pay what he saw as the outrageously inflated prices of a professional plumber, he went on-line and learnt to do it all himself. He plumbed everything in — installed the toilet, a power shower, basin and bath; he even did the tiling himself. He'd been the same with his new computer. Within a very short time, he'd become a master of its state-of-the-art workings. He even taught himself to produce a website trumpeting his own skills and accomplishments. 'In case I ever decide to set up on my own,' he'd explained when Tory asked him why he'd done that. Everything had to be accomplished by him so that people would admire him and see how clever and versatile he was. Another indication, Tory now wondered, of a disturbed mind or personality? It was narcissism, she'd once read. The unnatural and obsessive need for attention and praise.

She walked into the kitchen and glanced nervously around. Then she put Millie down and opened one of the cupboards, the one where she stored their food. The contents had once again been rearranged: cans in perfectly symmetrical rows from front to back according to their contents; packets in another row; boxes the same. She then opened the cutlery drawer: everything was in its rightful place. Even the tea towel, which she'd left draped across the worktop, was hanging on its rail.

There was no further doubt in her mind. This was Stuart's way of letting her know he was here in Compton Cross — and he had access to her home any time he wanted. But, as she'd already concluded, he couldn't be staying in the village. A stranger would quickly be noticed, and questions asked as to his identity. And Tory, working at a checkout as she did, would have been quizzed for sure as to whether she knew who the new incomer was. Which all seemed to point towards Stuart having been the snooper, hiding beneath the cover of darkness, disguised by means of a hat pulled low over his head as he attempted to find out exactly where she was. Thank goodness he hadn't walked into the mini-market; he couldn't have helped but see her, and who knew what would have happened then. There could well have been some sort of scene. But then again, he wouldn't have expected her to be sitting at a checkout, so wouldn't have bothered looking inside one of the shops for her. She shivered then as fear spiralled its way through her.

'Go up to your bedroom, Millie, and get those wet things off.' Millie, her tears dried, ran out of the room. Tory heard the thump of her small feet as she raced up the stairs. She heard her open her door, and then her alarmed voice shouting once more, 'Mummy, Mummy ...'

Oh no. Was Stuart actually here inside the house, waiting for them? She raced up the stairs and into the bedroom, and saw what had so startled Millie.

The normal mess of toys and books lying around had gone. Everything was in its rightful place. Millie's two dolls and her teddy were arranged on the bed, propped up stiffly against the pillows, their glassy eyes staring straight at Tory as she walked into the room. Games were back in their boxes and books were stacked neatly on a shelf. All the other toys were back in their box in the corner of the room. The bed was made, Millie's dressing gown was hung on its hook on the door, and the clothes that they'd left lying haphazardly on the bed in their haste that morning had gone. Tory opened the wardrobe door and saw them all neatly back on their hangers and shelves.

'Daddy's here,' Millie said. 'He's tidied up for me.' A wary expression came over her face. 'Will he smack me for being untidy?' She looked around the room. 'Where is he? Is he hiding?'

'I don't think so. I don't know where he is.'

Tory hastened into her own room. That, too, had been tidied. Like Millie's room, clothes she'd left lying on the bed had been hung up in the wardrobe or stored, neatly folded into drawers. The room was empty, however. The bathroom was the same. Towels hung perfectly straight, the bar of soap positioned squarely in its appointed place on the wash basin, bathmat perfectly placed alongside the bath waiting for a pair of wet feet.

With her heart beating like a drum, she went quietly down the stairs and crept into the sitting room. It, too, was empty.

She made a decision. She'd call the police. Even if he'd not actually broken in, he'd most certainly been inside, un-invited. She typed out the number of the emergency services and asked for the police, then related exactly what had happened and detailed who she thought was responsible for it all. The person she spoke to told her that someone would be with her within an hour, which gave her enough time to put Millie to bed. She didn't want her around when the police arrived. Their presence, and the questions they'd be bound to ask, would only upset her even more than she already was.

They duly turned up and she repeated all that she'd told the call handler on the phone. They looked around, but with no real evidence, they told her, there wasn't much they could do. 'There's no sign that he's broken in, there's no damage, and with nothing missing, he's not officially committed a crime. You say you believe it was your husband, and he hasn't taken anything, he's just tidied up. Could he have got hold of a key somehow?'

'Um — oh, I hadn't thought.' She hurried across to the small bureau in the corner of the sitting room where she kept the spare. It had gone.

'The spare key's gone!' she cried. Why hadn't she checked that before now? 'He must have managed to gain entry initially and helped himself to the key.'

She recalled the first disturbing incident when the kitchen window had been open. That had to have been the night he'd first got into the cottage. He'd picked the front door lock, there was no other explanation. He'd then searched for and found the spare key, before closing the cupboard door deliberately loudly enough that she'd hear it, and slipped out again, leaving her to go downstairs and discover the rearranged contents and the open window. He'd know she'd suspect it was him behind it, and that from then on she'd live in fear. And since then, he'd been able to simply let himself in any time and do whatever he wanted.

'If I were you, Mrs Matthieson, I'd get your lock changed, pronto. Maybe fix a bolt to the back door as well. Window locks and a burglar alarm might be advisable, too. You don't seem to have either.'

'No, it's a rented property, so ...' She shrugged. She certainly couldn't afford an alarm, or even window locks, come to that. 'Well, thank you for coming.'

'I'm sorry, but there's really not much we can do. We don't have the resources anymore to set up a watch.'

'I understand.'

It had been a waste of time reporting it all. She'd have to take her own precautions. She would get the front door lock changed as quickly as she could, and then inform the landlord. Maybe he'd even pay for the work, and new lock. She'd also fix a bolt on the back door.

First thing next morning, she rang a local locksmith. He agreed, as it was an emergency, to come immediately and fit the new lock.

★   ★   ★

All in all, Tory's spirits were at a very low ebb. Which must have been why, when Damien Grey rang her on her afternoon off a couple of days later and asked her out that same evening, she instantly agreed. Anything to banish thoughts of what was happening to her. And really, how bad could it be?

'Wow!' he said. 'I thought it was such a long shot, I almost didn't ring you. After all, you refused point-blank when I first suggested taking you out. What changed your mind?'

'I've had a couple of really bad days,' she lightly remarked, 'and I need to get out.'

'Might I ask what's happened?'

'Oh, nothing you'd want to know about, believe me.'

'Try me.'

'No, really. It's sorted now anyway — at least, I hope it is.'

'Okay. Have it your own way.' He paused, then said, 'There's a very good restaurant in Ludlow. Do you fancy trying it?'

'Oh yes,' she enthusiastically replied. 'But — will the roads be passable?' The snow was stubbornly hanging around, though the main roads were more or less clear.

'I'm sure they will, but the Range Rover will cope with them in any case. Seven-thirty suit you? I'll pick you up, of course.'

'Um — yes, but I need to ring Julia to make sure she can have Millie for the night. Can I ring you back to confirm that time?'

'Yeah, sure. You have my number on the card I gave you.'

She rang Julia immediately. 'Of course

I'll have Millie,' her friend said. 'I'll come and fetch her if you like. My car's good in the snow.' She was the proud owner of a four-wheel drive vehicle, paid for by her ex, naturally. She'd described it as the direct result of his guilt trip over leaving her and Megan. 'Where are you going? Somewhere nice?'

'A restaurant in Ludlow.'

'Blimey! Sounds posh. Let me guess. It's Damien Grey — am I right?'

'You are,' Tory reluctantly confirmed. Knowing Julia, she'd have a lot more to say upon learning that. She was swiftly proved right.

'You jammy beggar! How in hell's name have you managed that? And I thought he wasn't your type,' she scoffed. 'Mind you, I could see he fancied you something rotten.'

'He just rang out of the blue. A couple of minutes ago, actually.'

'Well, I'm deeply envious. I'd give my eye teeth to go out with him.'

'I gathered that,' Tory told her, grinning to herself. 'The eyelash-fluttering sort of gave the game away.'

Julia laughed. 'That obvious, was I? Shame it didn't work. What time are you going?'

'He's picking me up at seven-thirty.'

'Right. I'll come for Millie at seven then.'

★ ★ ★

With that settled and Millie taken care of, all Tory had to contend with was the tricky decision of what to wear. She was quite sure that Damien Grey was accustomed to women who only dressed in the smartest and most expensive designer wear. And she had nothing that would come anywhere near to equalling that.

She went through her entire wardrobe, which was worryingly inadequate. She'd been forced to leave quite a lot of clothes behind when she fled — not that she'd had any designer garments, in any case.

In the end she plumped for a pair of silky navy-blue trousers and the fitted cream and navy tunic top that went with it. However, once on, she eyed the top doubtfully. It was cut fairly low, as well as being extremely close-fitting. She frowned. Had it always been like that? Or had she put on weight? A scarf, that was what she needed; decoratively draped, it would conceal the abundance of flesh on view. And she had the very one: pale blue and freckled with the odd sequin.

She went to the chest of drawers and opened the top one where she kept her collection of scarves and hats. She went through the items one by one as she searched for it. She frowned. It wasn't there. She moved across to the dressing table and opened that drawer. It wasn't there either. She returned to the chest of drawers, pulled everything out and heaped it all on the bed. The scarf had vanished. Could she have left it behind? No, she remembered packing it.

Stuart. He must have taken it. It was her favourite, the one she wore most often — which he knew very well. It turned a plain outfit into something a bit more exotic. It was yet another tactic to let her know he had access to her home and all that she owned, whenever he wanted.

The doorbell rang, heralding Julia's arrival. Tory ran down the stairs calling, 'Millie, Auntie Julia's here. Bring your bag with you.' She opened the door and there was her friend.

'Wow!' Julia exclaimed. 'You're giving him an eyeful then, I see.'

'I've been trying to find a scarf to drape. I'll have to change,' Tory wailed. But into what? She had nothing else remotely suitable for dining in an upmarket restaurant. If only she hadn't had to leave so many of her belongings behind.

'No, don't do that,' Julia said. 'You look gorgeous.'

Tory pulled a face and tried to yank the revealing neckline higher. It was useless.

'What shall I do?' She was verging on panic by this time. 'I can't find the scarf that goes with it. It's vanished.' For a split second she was tempted to tell Julia everything, but she didn't have time.

'Millie,' she shouted again, 'come on.'

Millie appeared at the top of the stairs, bag trailing behind her on the floor as she said, 'Hello, Auntie Julia.'

'Hello, sweet pea.'

'Where's Megan?'

'In the car, waiting for you. She's so excited you're coming for a sleepover. Now, are you all set?'

'No. Mummy, I can't find my colouring book. It's the one we bought the other day. I've looked everywhere. Daddy must have taken it when he tidied up.' Her bottom lip quivered.

'Never mind now, darling,' Tory told her, steadfastly ignoring Julia's quizzical expression. 'We'll find it tomorrow.' But she couldn't help wondering what else he'd helped himself to. 'If not, we'll buy another one. Now, off you go.'

As she opened the front door to let Julia and Millie out, a black Range Rover drew up at the kerb right behind Julia's car. She closed her eyes momentarily. Julia would now have a field day.

Never one to disappoint, her friend

instantly cried, 'I couldn't have timed this better if I'd tried. Hello, Damien,' she said as he approached the door.

'Hello, Julia. Millie.' His gaze left Julia almost immediately and riveted itself upon Tory.

'I'm almost ready. Come in,' Tory invited him. 'Bye, Julia,' she pointedly added before bending down to bestow a warm kiss upon Millie's uplifted cheek. 'Bye, precious. Be good for Auntie Julia.'

'I'm always good,' Millie indignantly told her.

Tory glanced up and saw Damien grinning broadly down at the small girl. 'Atta girl,' he then said before crouching before her and asking, 'And how's my favourite princess?'

Millie giggled. 'I'm not a princess.'

'You are in my eyes.'

'I can't find my new colouring book.' She frowned at him. 'I think my daddy took it.'

Tory sensed rather than saw Damien stiffen, but she definitely saw him glance up at her.

'Millie,' she swiftly put in, 'Auntie Julia's waiting to go.'

'Oh, there's no rush,' Julia assured her. 'It's only a quarter to seven. You're early, Damien. Keen, obviously!' And she gave a smirk. 'Well, my children, have a wonderful time, won't you? I'll see you tomorrow after work, Tory. You can tell me all about your evening then,' she smoothly concluded, with a sly wink.

Once the two of them had gone, Damien stepped inside the house. For a second time, he subjected Tory to his narrow-eyed and gleaming gaze. 'You look delicious. Good enough to eat, in fact.' He then grinned at the blush that instantly flamed on her face.

She decided not to encourage him, and said instead, 'It's not too dressy?'

'It's perfect.' He appeared to be pointedly not looking in the direction of her low neckline.

'Okay.' She gave a muted sigh. 'Come into the sitting room while I go up and apply the finishing touches.'

'You look very finished to me,' he

murmured, the wicked gleam still present in his eyes.

'Um — well, just excuse me for one moment.' She fled from the room, her pulse threatening to go into hyperdrive as she did so. Oh, good grief, how was she going to cope with him? She'd never encountered a man quite like him before. He was making no secret of his desire for her, none at all. Not even Stuart, in the early days of their relationship, had been quite so outspoken. Was this evening going to turn out to be a huge, huge mistake?

She went into her bedroom and began to work on her hair, which proved an almost impossible task. Her fingers quivered as she attempted to pile the mass of curls high at the back of her head. She did manage to pin them in place, sort of, deliberately leaving some tendrils free on either side to soften the effect and frame her face. They'd only drop down anyway, so she might as well pre-empt things. She then sprayed a load of hair lacquer all over it, hoping it would hold everything in place for the entire evening.

Now, a necklace. She had to find something; anything. None of her other scarves were suitable for evening wear. She scrabbled through her jewellery box and finally found a chunky necklace she'd forgotten she had. That would go some way towards distracting Damien's glances. At least, she hoped so. She quickly fastened it, but it barely concealed the inches of flesh that were on display. Oh well, she didn't have time to change, and there was nothing more she could do; she'd have to brazen it out. She dragged a jacket from the wardrobe, slipped her feet into a pair of high-heeled shoes, sprayed some perfume, and she was done.

She went back downstairs, her heartbeat still manic. Desperately trying to appear calm and composed, and failing miserably, she suspected, she strolled into the sitting room, only to find Damien on the prowl. He was holding a framed photograph of herself, Stuart, and Millie at twelve months old.

He swivelled his head so that he was looking straight at her, which meant she didn't miss his expression of surprise at the sight of her hair. However, as he made no comment, she had no idea whether he approved or not. Not that his opinion mattered. She'd given up dressing purely to please a man.

'Your husband?'

She nodded.

He frowned. 'So — has he been visiting you? I was under the impression that it was all over between you — until Millie mentioned that her father might have taken a colouring book.'

'It is all over. Absolutely. It's just that she's lost a colouring book, and ...' She shrugged. 'Stuart was a great one for tidying things away, so she got into the habit of blaming him for anything she couldn't find.' She gave a weak smile. She wasn't comfortable with any sort of a lie; never had been. Her expression would invariably give her away. She just hoped it wasn't doing that now.

'He hasn't been here then, visiting?'

'Good heavens, no.'

However, as Damien's frown remained

firmly in place, she suspected he didn't believe her. She felt her cheeks beginning to warm again. And, from the way his eyes narrowed at her, she knew he'd noticed. Was there anything this man didn't see? Her low neckline, her hair, her blush. The evening, she concluded, was going to be an ordeal. She had so much to hide, so much she didn't want to talk about.

'Shall we go?' she suggested. Anything to remove that penetrating gaze from her flushed face. It was becoming all too apparent that Damien Grey would be a hard man to fool, and she had impulsively agreed to spend the entire evening alone with him. What the hell had she been thinking of?

8

Within moments, they were on their way to Ludlow. Tory had been there once before as a child with her parents, as she had to Compton Cross. She had vague memories of an ancient castle and a large square where, apparently, special events were held. Fairs, that sort of thing. She also remembered a lot of black-timbered buildings lining narrow, cobbled streets.

'So what have you been up to today?' Damien asked. 'As you were at home when I phoned, I presume you've had the day off?'

'Afternoon. I worked this morning. The free time gave me a chance to catch up on some chores. I'm not the world's most fastidious housekeeper, I'm afraid.'

'Did Millie manage to build her snow-man after all?'

'Yes, the next morning. It didn't last long though.' She stopped talking abruptly.

As it was, she'd said enough to warrant further questions. He'd be bound to want to know what happened. It hadn't been warm enough for the snowman to melt.

And sure enough, he instantly asked, 'Oh? Why not?'

She might as well tell him. 'We got home that evening to find it in pieces all over the lawn.'

'Really? How did that happen?'

'No idea. Maybe someone got into the garden and smashed it up. Kids; a dog, perhaps.' Now, she was sounding ridiculous. No dog would have scaled a high fence. And kids? She was sure they'd have found such a feat impossible as well.

Damien echoed her thoughts, not bothering to conceal his scepticism. 'Are either of those things likely? Don't those houses back onto fields? And the gardens must be fenced in, surely? There are cows in there at certain times of the year.'

How did he know that?

'I know John Campbell,' he went on, clearly having noticed her quizzical look. 'The chap who owns the field.'

'I see. The gardens are fenced, yes, but I suppose someone could have got into the field and climbed over.' Again, she was being ridiculous. Who the blazes would bother getting into a field and climbing a fence just to smash a child's snowman to pieces? But she didn't know what else to say. And, more to the point, why on earth had she even told him what had happened in the first place?

'Who would have done such a thing?' He was looking angry now. 'Millie must have been terribly disappointed.'

'Yes, she was, but we did manage to build another small one this afternoon between the chores.'

She directed her gaze through the side window and allowed the conversation to lapse. To her relief, Damien followed suit, and within a very short time they'd reached Ludlow and were walking into the restaurant.

The town was exactly as Tory remembered it, even down to the restaurant being an ancient one, heavily beamed, with small leaded windows, and the upper floor leaning perilously far out over the pavement. A genuine relic of Tudor times.

Once they were inside, a maître d' greeted them warmly. 'Mr Grey? So nice to see you. I believe you said when you booked that you've visited us before?'

'I have, yes. A couple of times.'

'I'm so glad you decided to return.'

Tory found herself wondering who he'd brought with him those other times. Maddeningly, he guessed the direction of her thoughts.

'I came with a friend last time, and my parents the time before,' he smoothly told her.

'How nice,' she couldn't resist retorting. 'A close friend, was it?'

'If you mean a woman, then yes. I don't see her anymore.'

'No girlfriend at the moment then?' she murmured as they followed the maître d' to a secluded table laid for two and set up in the corner of the room, close to a log fire. She was struggling to suppress her feelings of — what? Jealousy? It certainly felt like it.

'No, although I'm hoping that's about to change.'

He meant her. The expression in his eyes left her in no doubt about that. She gasped softly, the breath snagging in her throat at the mere thought of a relationship with this handsome man. Images of being held in his arms, of his mouth being pressed to hers, filled her head. It was mind-blowing. In an effort to change the direction the conversation was taking, she said, 'Oh, good, a log fire. I'm freezing.'

'We can't have that, can we?' he laughed throatily. 'I'll have to see what I can do to warm you up.'

Those simple words conjured up even more disturbing images, and yet again she felt her cheeks warming.

★   ★   ★

The meal they ate was the best Tory had ever had, and she relished every mouthful. Even the conversation turned out to be enjoyable, as she found out a lot more about her companion.

'Tell me about your work,' she'd begun, as their starters were placed before them. 'I'm sure it's much more interesting than mine. More challenging,' she added, in a deliberate reminder of his words to her on their first encounter.

If he discerned her reference to his derision of her work, he gave no indication of it. 'Well, I dabble in a lot of things. I play the stock market; I also buy up failing businesses and restore them to profit before selling them on. A couple of months ago, I invested in an IT outfit that designs bespoke computer programs. They also design websites. That's doing rather well, although it is early days yet.'

'So you're an entrepreneur?'

'I suppose so.'

'Tell me a bit about your family.'

He looked quite happy to answer her questions, which did surprise her. 'Two parents and a sister, Carolyn, married to Matt. She's a nurse, he's a GP.'

'In Compton Cross?'

'Yes. My whole family live there. In fact, we've never lived anywhere else.

That's why I decided to buy Compton Court when it came onto the market. I'd been in an apartment on the other side of the village up until then.'

'How long have you lived there?'

'Seven or eight months or so. I'm still settling in. There's a great deal to do on the refurbishment side. The previous owners let it go a bit.'

'Sounds expensive.' It was a wonder Julia hadn't mentioned this. She seemed to be aware of most things that went on in Compton Cross, and wasn't averse to gossiping about them.

'It is, so I'm taking it slowly.'

There was something else bothering her. 'What's your brother-in-law's name?' she asked, slightly uneasily.

'Matt Lewis. Don't tell me he's your doctor.'

'He is, actually,' and she felt a pang of concern about that — the years with Stuart had left their mark on her. Still, all doctors were bound by confidentiality laws, so it was highly unlikely he'd discuss her with his brother-in-law.

'Don't look so worried. By all accounts, he's very good. Now, enough about me and mine. How about you? Where are you from? What family do you have?'

She told him all that she felt able to, glossing over her drunken bully of a father and her spoilt sister. The only one she felt able to talk about freely was her mother. 'She's worked her way up to the position of manager of a small dress shop, so she could always get a discount for me on any clothes that I wanted. Which was extremely welcome!' She slanted a grin at him.

He hesitated, drawing a steadying breath, before asking, 'And your husband?'

She'd been waiting for this; dreading it, in fact. Again, she intended to keep the details to a bare minimum. 'We're separated.'

'Not divorced?' He arched a quizzical eyebrow at her.

'No, not yet.'

He reclined back into his seat and twiddled the stem of his wineglass with his fingers. He had recovered his colour

and his composure was back to normal.
'Why not?'

She felt like saying, *Don't hold back,
will you?* But, of course, she didn't.
'There hasn't been time,' she prevari-
cated. 'And Stuart's being … difficult.'
There was an understatement, if ever
she'd heard one.

Damien didn't speak for a long
moment, and his expression was a specu-
lative one. Tory swallowed nervously.
Now what was coming? However, all he
said was, 'And how does Millie feel about
it all? I mean, she talks about him. Does
she see him?'

Tory simply shook her head.

'That seems a little hard on her. How
long have you been separated?'

'It'll be six months next week.'

'Is that why you came here? To get
away from him?'

She nodded.

He continued to stare at her, his eyes
narrowed to slits. 'Why is that? Are you
afraid he'll bother you?'

She didn't reply. She simply shook her

head. Stuart's behaviour during the past couple of weeks couldn't be described as bothering her. It was much, much worse than that. It felt more like a campaign of fear and intimidation. But she couldn't tell Damien that. She didn't know him well enough. She began to fidget beneath the intensity of his gaze. It was as if he could see right inside her, and it wasn't a comfortable sensation.

'And Millie doesn't see him? He doesn't visit her?'

Again, she shook her head.

'Yet she clearly thought he'd been to the cottage and taken her book?'

'I don't know why she thought that. As I said earlier, it must be because she was accustomed to him tidying up for her. It was her way of explaining its disappearance. I'm sure she's left it somewhere. At Julia's maybe,' she lightly said. 'It'll turn up.'

'She clearly misses him. Whose decision was it for her not to see him?'

'It was a joint decision.' She felt the revealing colour creeping up her face.

Exasperation made itself felt. Other people seemed to have no problem telling lies — well, as far as she knew anyway. Because, let's face it, if they were good at it, she wouldn't realise what they were doing, would she?

'A rather cruel one, wouldn't you say?'

'We decided it would be best that way. For Millie.' She was tempted to ask, *And what business is it of yours, anyway? You know absolutely nothing about it.* But she thought better of it. Instead she met his gaze, her expression — she hoped — one of defiance.

But whatever he'd made of her look, heavy lids lowered even further over his eyes until they were almost closed. 'Is there something you're not telling me?'

That did it. Her temper flared, as it was prone to do when she found herself in a situation like this one. Who did he think he was, interrogating her in such a fashion? She was starting to regret coming out with him.

'Quite a lot,' she snapped, 'but as we've only just met I don't think full disclosure would be appropriate.'

His eyes widened at that and then darkened once more, with what closely resembled anger. However, as the expression immediately vanished again, she couldn't be sure. Maybe she'd imagined it? Nonetheless, it had been a scary reminder of the look Stuart always had, right before he struck her.

All Damien said, though, was a light, 'Point taken.'

The conversation moved on after that as they reverted to companionable conversation and discussed their individual lives in general. But Tory sensed he was dissatisfied with her responses, guessing she was holding quite a lot back. Mentally, she shrugged. She couldn't help that. She didn't know him anywhere near enough to confide the truth. No matter that she was deeply attracted to him. There, she'd admitted it.

She expelled a long, shuddering breath as she asked herself how she could possibly become involved romantically with one man while still married to another. It went against every principle that she held. But more than that — suppose Stuart found out she was seeing someone? How would he react? With more violence?

She shouldn't have agreed to come out with Damien. It wasn't fair to him, encouraging him to anticipate some sort of relationship with her when she knew that wasn't possible, not in her present situation.

And then something else occurred to her. Something even more disturbing. Suppose Stuart had been outside that evening, standing nearby, unseen in the darkness, watching the cottage? He'd have seen her leaving with another man. Her heart lurched in her breast. He could already be planning some sort of retaliation or punishment.

By the time they left the restaurant, it was snowing again. 'Oh no,' Tory wailed. This was the final straw. She had enough on her plate to worry about without having to be concerned about getting home. And suppose Stuart was outside the cottage waiting for them? She felt sick, and her stomach churned violently. She should never have come. She lifted a hand to her forehead. Her skin was burning, and it wasn't the result of a blush.

'Don't worry.' Damien sounded concerned. He'd clearly noticed her abrupt change of mood. 'There's not much the Range Rover won't cope with.'

'Let's hope you're right.' Her tone was waspish. She felt him dart another glance towards her. He must be wondering what the hell had happened; what had changed her mood from one of friendliness to one of ill-tempered tetchiness.

And, of course, he was right. She should have known he would be. The vehicle ploughed through the thickly falling snow, and they were soon pulling up in front of Primrose Cottage.

Damien turned off the engine and half-turned to look at her. Tory didn't notice at first, being too engrossed in staring around, her entire being filled with a dreadful anxiety as she searched for a glimpse of Stuart. But he wasn't anywhere to be seen, and in any case, she mustn't let his actions dictate what she did. She had to be strong; show him she was her own woman and wouldn't be intimidated into doing what he wanted. Otherwise, what would have been the point of leaving him? And, more to the point, on a night like this, with snow falling, would he really be lying in wait? She doubted it.

She turned to Damien and said, 'Would you like to come inside and have a coffee?'

But she couldn't stop herself glancing up and down the road just once more in case Stuart should be there, lurking in the shadows. When there was still no sign of him, she swivelled back to face Damien. He was watching her intently.

'Looking for someone?' he asked.

'No. Why would I be?'

He tilted his head to one side. 'You tell me.'

'There's nothing to tell. So,' she asked again, 'do you want to come in?' All of a sudden she was breathless at the mere notion of him in the house alone with her.

'Thank you, that would be a perfect ending to a perfect evening,' he murmured throatily.

Tory felt her pulse leap. Shakily, she climbed from the car. Although it was snowing, it wasn't snowing as heavily here as it had been in Ludlow. Nonetheless, Damien gallantly took hold of her arm to escort her across the treacherous pavement and along the drive to her front door. She slid the key into the new lock. It turned smoothly. She wondered then whether Stuart had attempted to get in while she'd been out. If he had, he would have received a shock. She just hoped he hadn't managed to pick the lock, as he must have done that first time — though that would be more difficult now. She'd had a mortice lock fitted, which the locksmith had assured her would be much harder, if not impossible, to tamper with.

'I'll put the kettle on,' she said, 'if you'd like to put a match to the fire in the sitting room. You'll find a box on the mantelpiece.'

'Sure,' he said, and he strode across

the small hallway, his long legs covering it in three strides. It took Tory twice as many as that.

She made the coffee and placed the cafetiere and both cups on a tray along with cream and sugar, before carrying it into the sitting room, all the while ignoring the mad pounding of her heartbeat.

Damien, on the other hand, hadn't wasted any time making himself at home. He sat, the picture of total ease, in the corner of the settee, one elbow propped on the arm, his legs stretched out before him, his ankles crossed.

She placed the tray on a low table and poured the coffee, somehow managing to not spill it. Then, after handing him one of the cups, she made her way to the armchair that sat immediately opposite.

He watched her, a half-smile on his lips. 'I don't bite, you know,' he said in a low voice. 'Not unless provoked.' Amusement glinted at her now.

'I'm sure you don't,' she primly responded.

'So come and sit here with me, then,'

he said, and patted the cushion alongside him. He then placed his cup onto the table before holding out a hand to her and saying, 'Please.'

Acutely uncertain as to the wisdom of what she was about to do, she sat down, pressing herself as far into the opposite corner as she could get without actually perching on the arm.

He bent forward and lifted his cup once more. 'Are you always like this?'

'Like what?' she stammered.

'Distant; edgy.'

'I'm not edgy.' She tried a snort of amusement, only to fail miserably. It had erupted like a strangulated sneeze. Whatever must he be thinking of her? She was behaving with all the twitchy nervousness of an adolescent girl. 'Why would I be?'

But whatever he was thinking, all he said was, 'You tell me.' Having finished his coffee, without removing his gaze from her he replaced the empty cup on the table. Tory deliberately took her time drinking hers. He waited, not speaking, until in the end she had no option but to also put her cup down.

'I'm not going to jump on you, you know.'

'I know.' She swallowed nervously.

'Do you? So why don't you move a little closer?'

She inched towards him, and felt several strands of hair drop down from the loose knot she'd so painstakingly arranged earlier. Vexed, she tried to push them back up.

'Leave them,' said Damien softly. 'I like the disordered look. And you have beautiful hair. You must know how attracted I am to you, Tory,' he went on. He put a finger beneath her chin and tilted her face up to his.

More hair worked loose. This time, she left it. 'Are you?'

'Yes.' He spoke so low she could barely hear him. 'You are an extremely lovely woman, and I want ...' He stopped himself then, to better arrange his words. 'I hope we can get to know each other a little better.'

Their lips were only inches apart now. His warm breath feathered the skin of her face. The scent of his aftershave filled her nostrils. The sheer magnetism of him fanned her senses into an unbearably heightened awareness of how deeply she was attracted to him. Her head began to spin as her breathing quickened and her heartbeat raced.

He closed the small gap between them and captured her lips with his. All Tory could muster then was a tiny moan as she surrendered to what was beginning to feel inevitable, and had been since the first time he'd stood over her, eyes gleaming with what she now understood to be heated desire.

9

Damien threaded the fingers of his hand through her hair, freeing it to tumble down about her shoulders. He grasped a silky handful and brought it to his face, inhaling the perfume she'd sprayed earlier. 'You smell gorgeous.' He gently kissed her eyelids, then her arched throat.

She gave an involuntary gasp. Every inch of her throbbed with longing, desire, passion. Her hands crept up to entwine at the back of his neck.

'Oh God, Tory,' he groaned.

Reality cut through the desire. What was she doing? Hadn't she learnt anything from the past years? She'd sworn never to allow another man into her life. To never allow another man to become important to her, to have power over her. She valued her hard-won freedom and independence too much.

'No, no. Stop.' She dragged her arms

from his shoulders and pushed him away. 'Please, don't.' She struggled to her feet and stood, hunched and trembling, both arms folded across her middle in an overtly defensive stance. Unlike Stuart, Damien made no attempt to stop her. He simply gazed up at her, his brow knotting.

'What's wrong?' he quietly asked. 'Did I hurt you?'

'Yes. No. It's everything. I can't do this. I'm sorry.'

Visibly struggling to gather his thoughts, Damien got to his feet as well, and stood facing her.

'Me too,' he finally said. 'I thought we both felt the same. I can't pretend to understand what's going on right now. Can you try and explain?'

'I have to think of Millie,' she said, rather unconvincingly.

'Are you sure it's Millie on your mind, and not your husband?'

Tory raised her gaze defiantly. 'That's part of it,' she said, not untruthfully.

'He left you, and you're not over him — is that it?' said Damien, trying to understand.

'He didn't leave me; I left him. For my own peace of mind, and my and Millie's safety,' she blurted, telling him far more than she wanted to. She'd never see him again after this evening's debacle.

He went completely still. 'What do you mean?' he demanded. 'Your safety? What did he do to you?' His jaw hardened as his gaze darkened. 'Was he violent? Is that it? Did he hit Millie?'

Oh, good grief, now she'd done it. What the hell had possessed her? 'Please. Just go. I don't want to talk about it. I don't want any trouble. Please.'

'Trouble? Are you frightened of me, is that it? Frightened of men? Because of him?'

'Will you just go? I don't want to see you again. I can't.'

'Tory.' His face looked carved from granite. 'If he was abusing you ...'

Tears stung her eyes and overflowed to stream down her face. She made no move to wipe them away. He moved towards her, his arms reaching for her. As much as she yearned for him to hold her, Tory

148

did the only thing she could. She backed away, holding her hands out in front of her, unequivocally warding him off. 'Just go,' she reiterated. 'This isn't going to work; it can't work.'

He didn't respond to that, other than to simply gaze at her, his eyes gentle. 'I meant what I said.' His voice was low. 'I still hope to get to know you. I want you. You must know that. And I thought you wanted me. I still do think that. I can't believe I got that entirely wrong.' He paused, giving her the opportunity to say something. But when she didn't, he went on. 'If you ever feel threatened in any way, you or Millie, you call me. Will you promise me that?'

She didn't answer. How could she drag anyone else into this, much less another man? If Stuart got wind of her involvement with someone else, she couldn't answer for his actions. She didn't know what he'd do. She had come to the conclusion that her husband had serious mental problems, and that could only mean trouble for all of them.

'Please go,' she quietly pleaded.

'Fine.' It was now his turn to hold his hands up in front of him. Only, in his case, it was a gesture of concession, not prevention. 'I'll go for now, but I'm not giving up on you, because I think … no, I know you want me too.'

She didn't respond. Couldn't respond. She was verging on complete disintegration into tears. Damien stared at her for another minute before turning and striding from the room. It wasn't until Tory heard the sound of the front door closing that she sank back down onto the settee. She covered her face with hands that shook, and gave way to the torrent of tears and heartbreak that had been threatening to rip her apart for the last few minutes.

Neither she nor Damien realised that a solitary figure, clothed entirely in black, had been standing on the opposite side of the road to Primrose Cottage, partially concealed by a thick tree trunk — watching, waiting, seemingly oblivious to the falling snow.

* ★ ★ ★

The following morning Tory overslept, only to wake to the sight of yet more snow. It was once more blanketing the ground. She sighed. Another difficult walk to work, made even more difficult by the intense and unremitting aching of her head. In fact, her entire body felt as if it had been battered, hard. She sneezed, and sneezed again. Her head throbbed even harder, and she reluctantly admitted that she didn't feel at all well.

She shivered and staggered back to bed, pulling the covers up over herself. Well, one thing she was sure about — she couldn't go to work feeling like this. She lifted her mobile phone and called the store to say she wouldn't be in. The manager, who was always in before anyone else — they all had the firm belief that it was solely to induce feelings of guilt in the rest of the staff — wasn't happy, but she accepted Tory's explanation.

'I trust you'll be okay tomorrow,' she

went on. 'You know how short-staffed we are at the moment.'

'Well I'll try, but I don't want to pass on whatever this is. I really feel ill. I'm sorry.'

'Okay. See how you are in the morning.'

She then rang Julia. 'Hi, it's me.' She sneezed hard, only just managing to avert her face from her phone in time.

'Hi there. Wow! You don't sound good.'

'No, I'm back in bed. I feel terrible.'

'Do you want me to come round?'

'No, not now. I'll try and sleep for a while and hope that does the trick. Could you bring Millie back this afternoon? I don't think I'll be up to collecting her.'

'Of course I will. And if you need anything, call me. Do you have plenty of tissues and paracetamol?'

'I think so. Thanks, Julia, you're a gem.'

With that done, Tory pulled the duvet back up around her neck and almost instantly fell into a deep sleep. When she awoke some hours later, she felt fractionally better, but still headachy and weak-limbed. She glanced at her bedside clock and saw that it was three o'clock. Millie would soon be back. Nursery finished at three-thirty. She'd better get up.

Shakily, she swung her legs out of bed and managed to stand. Her head instantly began to throb. She pulled on her dressing gown and limped down the stairs in search of some paracetamol. She found a packet with some still in it, so she downed a couple and drank a large glass of water.

When the doorbell chimed, she was stretched out on the settee. She dragged herself up, trying to pretend she wasn't feeling nauseous and dizzy, and went to open the door.

Julia and Millie stood on the step. No Megan. 'Ye Gods, you look like death, woman,' Julia cried.

'Thanks,' Tory bit out.

'Are you ill, Mummy?' Millie anxiously asked.

'A little bit, precious, but you don't need to worry. I'll soon be fine.' She glanced back at her friend. 'Are you coming in, or do you want to avoid the lurgy? Where's Megan?'

'I left her with my neighbour. I thought it best. And looking at you, I think I was right. Look, do you want me to keep Millie until tomorrow?'

'No, no,' Tory replied, taking in Millie's even more anxious expression. 'We'll be fine, won't we, sweetie? She's probably got it by now, anyway.'

'Well, if you're sure. I'll come in for a moment or two and make you a good strong cup of tea. You look as if you need one.'

Once that was accomplished and they were sat down sipping their drinks, Tory said to Millie, 'Go upstairs, love, for a while. I want to talk to Auntie Julia.'

'Okay, Mummy. I'll change my clothes. My trousers are wet from the snow.'

'Good girl.' She looked back at her friend and murmured, 'I need to talk to someone, Julia. I think I'll go mad if I don't.'

'I thought something was bothering you. You haven't been yourself lately. So go on — spill. Tell Auntie Julia all about it.'

154

So she did, holding nothing back: the abuse she'd suffered for so long; her desperate flight to escape Stuart; the suspicion that he was here somewhere; that he was the snooper, here to search for her; that he'd found her.

'But how did he know where to look?' Julia seemed genuinely appalled.

'My sister, Bella. She overheard Mum telling Dad the name of the town, that was all. I'd told Mum because I thought someone should know where I was, in case I was needed. Now that I think about it, it was pretty pointless, because I didn't give her my phone number, so she couldn't have got in touch with me if she needed to. I swore her to secrecy, but she told me that in the end Dad wore her down and she told him. Bella overheard her and apparently told Stuart.' She shrugged.

'So much for sisterly loyalty.'

'We've never really got along. She's only seventeen, and that ten-year gap ensured we were never close. She's always had a crush on Stuart, so she was probably trying to ingratiate herself with him. And now he's found me. He's been letting himself in here and tidying up, rearranging things in cupboards. He's obviously taken that book of Millie's that she couldn't find, as well as my missing scarf.'

'But how did he get in?'

Tory shrugged. 'I can only assume he picked the lock the first time. He's certainly clever enough. Then he found my spare key and helped himself. He's been in and out ever since.'

'Oh, Tory.' Julia looked upset.

'I've had a new lock fitted, so he can't do that anymore, but he'll find some way to get at me, I just know it.'

'Have you told the police about all of this?'

'Yeah. Two constables came round, but there's not a lot they can do, apparently. Haven't got the resources to find him and then keep a check on him. They advised me to change my lock and install a burglar alarm — the latter I can't afford.'

'Well, I'm glad you told me. Now, look

— if you're ever scared, you ring me. Promise?'

'I will. Thanks, Julia.' She smiled weakly. 'You won't repeat anything I've said, will you?'

Her friend looked offended. 'No. What do you take me for? Anyway, on a more cheery note, how did last evening go with the delicious Damien?' She gave a saucy smile and wiggled her eyebrows up and down.

Tory laughed. 'It was lovely. Wonderful food, wine ...'

'Is that all?' Julia looked genuinely disappointed. 'Didn't he make a move of any sort?'

As Tory had no intention of divulging the details, she contented herself with the single word, 'No.'

'Really? I find that hard to believe. He's got a reputation as a bit of a Casanova.'

'Not with me.'

★ ★ ★

Once Julia had left, Tory called Millie down. 'Come and have something to eat, darling.'

She managed to prepare the little girl a simple supper of scrambled eggs on toast before collapsing onto the settee in the sitting room.

'Aren't you having any supper, Mummy?' Millie asked.

'I'm giving my tummy a rest,' Tory told her.

Millie giggled. 'Is your tummy tired?'

Tory smiled at her. 'Something like that.'

'Can I have the TV on?' Millie asked, taking advantage of her mother's obvious weakened state of mind.

'Just for an hour, and then it's bedtime.'

'But Mummy, tomorrow's Saturday.'

'I know, but it's been a long day.'

'No, it hasn't.' Millie pouted at Tory, provoking a fond smile.

'You switch the TV on and I'll go and get myself a drink of water.'

'I'll come too. Can I have a biscuit?'

'Oh, okay, come along then.' She held

out her hand to Millie. They walked into the hallway.

'Oh look — a letter, Mummy.' Millie darted to the doormat and picked up the white envelope that lay there, then handed it to her mother.

Tory looked at it. It had clearly been hand-delivered, as there was no stamp. She frowned. 'VICTORIA' was printed in black ink on the front. With a sinking feeling, she tore it open and pulled out the single sheet of paper that lay within.

'Who's it from, Mummy?'

Tory swiftly read the words.

You won't get away with this, locking me out, keeping me from my daughter. She's mine. I demand to see her. If you don't let me, I won't answer for the consequences. Especially if you let that man into your home again.

'Is it from Daddy?' Millie asked, her clear gaze clouding as she did so.

'No. It's just a leaflet.' Tory scrunched it up and thrust it into her dressing gown pocket.

What was she to do? Just as she'd

feared, he'd been watching the cottage. How else could he know that Damien had been here? Something else struck her then. He must have only just pushed this through the letterbox, because it hadn't been there when she'd seen Julia out. Her heart lurched. Could he still be outside, waiting to see what she did? Waiting for her to open the door? And if she did, would he force his way in?

She darted into the sitting room. It had the only downstairs window that looked out onto the road. She pulled the curtain to one side and peered out. At first she couldn't see anyone; it was too dark, even taking into account the lying snow and the brightness it reflected in the moonlight. But then, as she stared along the road and back again, something stirred in the shadows across from the house. A figure stood beneath a tree, motionless for a full minute, before stretching an arm out in front of itself and pointing two fingers at her, mimicking the action of a gun firing a bullet. The figure then turned and strode away into the night.

It was Stuart. And his gesture had been a definite threat.

Tory let the curtain drop and stumbled back to where Millie was now sitting watching TV. She sank down by the side of her and held her close. Stuart would see Millie over her dead body. Bad choice of words, she grimly reflected. Because that was beginning to look like a distinct possibility. She shivered.

Millie looked up at her. 'Are you cold, Mummy?'

'Yes, darling, I am. Frozen.'

10

Tory tossed and turned for the entire night. She knew she couldn't leave Millie at Julia's the next day and go to work. She wouldn't have a moment's peace of mind. Stuart's threat was a genuine one, she had no doubt of that, and it couldn't be ignored. Should she call the police and show them the letter; tell them what had happened after she'd found it? But what could they do? They'd already made it perfectly clear they hadn't got the manpower to place a guard on her cottage. No, it was down to her to protect Millie and herself.

For the second time, she rang work and explained she still felt too ill to come in, which actually was perfectly true. Her head continued to ache and throb, and she suspected she was still running a temperature. The manager was even more displeased than she'd been the day before.

Nonetheless, eventually she accepted Tory's excuses, albeit grudgingly, and rang off with a curt, 'I trust I'll see you on Monday or we might have to review your position.'

That was all she needed, Tory thought wearily — to lose her job and income. She fed and dressed Millie and was just about to go to the bathroom and have a shower, hoping it would make her feel better, when the doorbell chimed. She froze. Could it be Stuart, come to verbally repeat his threats, or even to carry them out? She once again peered through the sitting-room window, and to her horror, saw Damien standing out there. She leapt back into the room. What the hell did he want? And with her looking like this.

She raked quivering fingers through her tangled hair, vainly trying to restore it to some semblance of order. She glanced down over her shabby dressing gown. It was one that she'd had since she was a teenager, and it was way too small for her, which meant it gaped all the way down the front, even when the belt was tied. And she was wearing an ancient, threadbare T-shirt underneath. What on earth would he think? Could she simply ignore him? However, when he rang again, longer and more insistently this time, she knew that wasn't an option. He must be aware she was inside. That had been a mistake; she should have resisted temptation and stayed away from it.

She walked into the hall and opened the door, just a couple of inches, hiding as much of herself behind it as she could.

'Tory,' he said. 'You look terrible.'

She looked back at him and sighed. Didn't that make her feel a whole lot better? 'Thanks,' she curtly responded. 'As you can see, I'm not quite ready to receive visitors.'

'Oh, is that why you're hiding behind the door?' he drawled. 'Can I come in anyway?'

'Why?' she bluntly demanded.

'I want to apologise.'

Reluctantly, she pulled the door wider.

'For the other evening,' he went on. 'I feel like I pushed you into telling me

... things you might not have wanted to.' He frowned. 'Are you ill? You're very pale.'

'I'm a bit under the weather, yes,' she grudgingly admitted.

'A bit under? I'd have said you were buried three feet deep. Look, do we have to do this on the doorstep? I'm beginning to attract a few stares.'

'Oh, okay. Come in then.'

'Thanks,' he retorted drily.

Resigning herself to the inevitable, Tory led the way into the sitting room, where Millie was engrossed in a favourite picture book.

'Damien!' she cried, getting up to run to him.

'Hello, Millie,' he greeted her, bending down to lift her up into his arms.

'Mummy's poorly,' she told him. 'Have you come to take care of her?'

'Well, if I can, and more importantly if she'll let me.' His glance met Tory's over Millie's head. 'You certainly look as if some TLC is desperately needed. Look.' He set Millie down onto the floor again.

'I can stay with Millie if you want to go back to bed. Have you called Matt?'

'Goodness, no. It's just a bug. It'll be gone by tomorrow, I'm sure.'

'Hey,' Millie suddenly cried, 'you can build a snowman with me.'

'I can do. If that's okay with Mummy?' He arched a quizzical eyebrow at Tory.

'Yes, I suppose so,' she wearily said. 'Are you sure you want to do that, though?' She looked at his clothes. He was wearing a rather smart pair of trousers and a very expensive-looking sweater. Cashmere, if she wasn't mistaken. His shoes also had the look of a designer-made pair.

'Oh, I've got my boots and a waterproof jacket in the back of the car. I keep them with me at all times at the moment.'

She regarded him. The mere idea of bed was suddenly irresistible. 'Well, if it's okay with you, it's okay with me.'

'He did promise,' Millie put in.

'You're right, I did, and I always try to keep my promises.' He grinned down at the little girl. 'Go and fetch your coat and boots, I'll fetch mine, and we'll get to it.'

But Tory had belatedly remembered Stuart's letter and his threat. What if he was somewhere watching the cottage right now and spotted Damien? Oh, blow him. She felt too ill to care, frankly. And really, what could he do, when all was said and done, in broad daylight?

With that decided, Tory gave in and thankfully retired to bed. She didn't sleep, though, mainly because of the sounds of merriment drifting up to her from the back garden, which her room backed onto. She got up at one point and looked out of the window. The two of them had built a massive snowman and now were pelting each other with snowballs. From the look of Damien, he was definitely coming off worse.

Millie glanced up and saw her, and called, 'Look, Mummy, I'm winning,' whereupon Damien descended on her with a roar and chased her round the garden. Millie screamed with delight.

'You can't catch me!' she yelled.

'You think?' Damien called back.

Tory laughed. He really was a nice man, at least as far as Millie was concerned. He'd make a wonderful father.

She sighed and returned to bed. She had to forget him. He wasn't for her. At least, not for as long as Stuart was around.

She was dozing intermittently when she became aware of her bedroom door quietly opening. 'Is that you, Millie?' she drowsily asked.

'No, it's me.'

She turned her head and saw Damien standing in the doorway. He was holding a tray upon which sat a bowl and a small vase with a tiny bunch of snowdrops from the garden in it.

'I don't suppose you had any breakfast, so I thought you might need something hot to eat. Chicken noodle soup. I rang my mother and she brought it round. She swears by it for the treatment of colds and 'flu. She's convinced it's some sort of miracle cure. For my part, I've always withheld judgement. Anyway, it can't do you any harm.'

Half-asleep still, Tory struggled to sit up. He rang his mother? Whatever did he say to her to make her deliver soup to a complete stranger? She was about to ask him that very question when she realised she was sitting up in the old T-shirt that she'd been wearing when he arrived. She lay back down and tugged the duvet up to just beneath her chin, her cheeks flaming with embarrassment.

'Oh, come on, Tory, I have seen a woman in bed before. At the age of thirty -four, it'd be pretty strange if I hadn't.'

'Quite,' she retorted. 'I did hear, though, you have a bit of a reputation as a Casanova.'

'Oh did you, now? Well, that's entirely undeserved.' He gave a low chuckle. 'Well, maybe not entirely. But it's only because I haven't been lucky enough to meet the right woman —'til now that is,' he softly concluded.

Surely he couldn't be planning to try and seduce her while she was lying in bed ill? She probably stank to high heaven. She'd been so sweaty and feverish. Surreptitiously, she bent her head and took a sniff. She breathed a small sigh of relief. She didn't.

Which was just as well, because he strode to the bed, laid the tray down on one side of her, then walked around to the other side to sit down.

'Are you strong enough to lift the spoon, or shall I feed you?' His lips twitched with amusement.

'I'm sure I can manage.'

'Pity.' He stared at her then, the amusement gone. 'I really am sorry about the other evening.'

She gazed up at him, her eyes wide and guileless. 'You mean for kissing me?'

'No, definitely not. I don't regret that for an instant. In fact —' He cocked his head as he regarded all that he could see of her — namely, her head.

'— I wouldn't mind repeating the experience.'

'I'm sure you wouldn't.' A thrill shot through her.

He leant down towards her.

'I'm probably contagious,' she murmured.

'So be it. A bout of 'flu would be well worth it in exchange for one of your kisses.' And he lowered his head to hers.

She parted her lips to him and slid her own arms up around his neck, pressing herself against him.

He gave a throaty moan, slipping his arms around her and gathering her even closer than she already was. Tory almost melted. She knew what she was doing was wrong, but she simply didn't care. She wanted him as much as he wanted her. He'd been right about that.

'Mummy.' It was Millie calling. 'Is Damien there?'

'Jees!' Damien jerked back and sprang up from the bed, letting Tory fall back onto the pillows.

She laughed. 'And that's one of the drawbacks of being a parent. You're liable to be interrupted at any moment.'

He grinned ruefully, and with more than a touch of embarrassment. 'Okay. To be continued, then. I'm coming, Millie,' he then called. 'Just giving Mummy some TLC.' And he arched an eyebrow at her, his eyes twinkling as he did so. It hadn't taken him long to regain his composure, she decided. He was clearly a practised lover, and was more than living up to his reputation.

He leant down to her and kissed her again. 'Drink your soup. It'll give you strength.' He dropped his voice. 'You're going to need it.'

And she did drink it, every last drop. It was delicious, and suddenly she felt heaps better. In fact, at that moment nothing seemed impossible. She'd get up, have a shower, and get dressed. She could return Damien's kindness in caring for Millie by cooking dinner for him.

But it wasn't to be. When she suggested it, he pulled a rueful face and said, 'I'd love to, but I have an important engagement this evening.'

It was now Tory's turn to pull a face.

'Don't look like that,' he murmured. 'It's a friend. We meet regularly, every month. He used to be my accountant.'

'I wasn't the least bit bothered about who you're meeting,' she instantly retaliated.

'Liar,' he softly said. He turned to Millie then. 'Well, Miss Millie, it's been a fantastic day. The best I've had in a long, long time.'

'We'll do it again,' she giggled. 'Mummy can join in next time. She missed all the fun.'

'Well,' he said, grinning at Tory, 'I wouldn't say that. She had a bit of fun of her own.'

Tory again pulled a face at him.

'But I'll never say no to a day spent in the company of two such beautiful ladies.'

'Silly.' Millie chuckled. 'I'm not a lady. I'm a girl.'

'So you are.' And he laughed. 'A gorgeous girl at that.' He picked her up and pressed kisses upon her cheek. 'I'll see you soon, little one, and that's a promise. Look after Mummy. I might pop in tomorrow and see how you both are, if that's OK?' He quirked an enquiring eyebrow at Tory and she nodded her agreement.

'Sure,' she said. 'Come to lunch. I'm cooking a roast.'

He frowned at that. 'Is that wise? You've been quite ill.'

'I'll be fine. I'm feeling much better.'

'Hmmm, must have been that chicken soup then — amongst other things.' And he gave a boldly lustful grin.

* * *

It was later that evening that Tory had reason to seriously reconsider her invitation to Damien for lunch the following day. Just after nine o'clock she heard a car pull up outside. Her heart leapt in her breast. Was it Damien? Had he rearranged his engagement?

Although she was tempted to run to the window, she sat quite still and waited for the chime of the doorbell. It didn't come. Instead, there was a loud banging on the wooden door. Tory jumped up, turned the sound down on the television and walked, somewhat hesitantly, into the hallway. Damien wouldn't bang on the door in such a manner. She stood still, her heartbeat quickening, a sense of misgiving beginning within her.

Almost at once, a man's voice shouted. 'I know you're in there. I saw him with Millie today. How dare you let another man in to play with her and deny me the same.'

She put both hands to her mouth. Oh God. She began to tremble.

'She's my daughter, not his. If he comes anywhere near either of you again, I'll kill him first and then you. Do you hear me? Is that clear?' There was another tremendous thump on the door before the sounds of a car starting up and driving off reached her, and then silence descended once again.

11

Tory slowly walked back into the sitting room, her thoughts whirling. Stuart had meant every word, she had no doubt about that. What should she do? She lifted a hand to her forehead. She couldn't think straight — and this time, it wasn't the result of her bout of 'flu.

The front doorbell chimed. She was so startled she practically leapt from the floor into the air. It couldn't be Stuart again, could it? She stood still, then crept to the window and peered out. It was one of her neighbours.

'Tory?' she heard him call. 'Are you okay?'

Tory ran to the door and tugged it open. 'John.'

'I heard shouting and banging. Are you okay? You don't look it.' He frowned anxiously at her.

'I'm recovering from a touch of 'flu but

I'm fine. It was just some nutter banging on the door. I ignored it. I thought it best.' She swallowed. Would he believe her?

He didn't. Instead, he regarded her with a deep scepticism. 'It certainly sounded most peculiar. He was threatening you, wasn't he? And I thought I heard Millie's name mentioned.'

'I don't know what it was, but it wasn't Millie. I can't imagine who he thought lived here.'

'Have you rung the police?'

'No. I don't think they'd be very interested.'

'Well, if it happens again, I think you should. I mean, we've heard tales of some sort of snooper. It might have been him. You can't be too careful.'

'Yes, I've heard the same thing. In fact, that's probably who it was. He's obviously deranged to be doing such things.'

She closed the door once he'd gone. She wasn't at all sure that he'd believed her. She returned to her armchair, almost fell into it, and leaned wearily back. What was she going to do? It was obvious Stuart was watching her every move; stalking her, in fact. And from the way he'd just behaved, she wouldn't put anything past him.

She jerked upright. If he was staking out the cottage, which it sounded as if he was, then he'd see Damien arrive in the morning. Heaven only knew what he'd do then. He'd have the entire road out wondering what was going on if he repeated his performance of a few moments ago. She had to stop Damien coming. She couldn't subject him to such embarrassment, and more importantly, she couldn't put him at risk of harm from Stuart. In fact, she had to end any possibility of a relationship between them.

Despair swamped her. Despite her resolve that she wouldn't allow Stuart to dictate how she lived her life, she acknowledged in that second that he'd won. She couldn't risk anyone getting hurt. And he'd sounded crazy enough to carry out his threats.

'Mummy?' It was Millie calling from

her bed. The banging and then the sound of voices must have woken her. 'Mummy, what's that noise?'

Tory ran up the stairs and straight into her daughter's room. 'It's okay, darling. It's nothing to be scared about.' She sat on the bed and gathered her small daughter into her arms.

'Was that Daddy shouting?' Her eyes were wide and full of fear.

'No, sweetie. It was some silly man outside.'

'Was he drunk? Was it peeping Tom?'

'Probably. Now then, there's nothing for you to worry about. You're safe in here. Come on, let's tuck you in.'

With Millie reassured and snuggled beneath her duvet once more, Tory went back downstairs and resorted to her customary panacea in times of trouble, a large mug of hot chocolate. She then found the card that Damien had given her and tapped out the number of his mobile phone. However, it went straight to voicemail.

She chewed at her bottom lip. She

couldn't end things between them with a message. It wasn't fair — not in the light of his kindness to her and Millie today. She'd ring him first thing in the morning. On no account must he be allowed to show up here.

★   ★   ★

Tory spent the better part of the night rehearsing over and over what she'd say to Damien, but nothing sounded right. He'd be furious with her. She couldn't stop herself repeatedly checking the digital numbers on her clock, as if that would make the hours pass more quickly. So when six o'clock came, she abandoned any attempt at sleeping and got up.

It was a relief when Millie came down and joined her at seven o'clock. Tory busied herself preparing breakfast, forcing herself to eat something, even if it was only a single slice of toast. By the time the kitchen clock reached nine, she could wait no longer. She retreated to her bedroom — she didn't want Millie to hear her — and typed Damien's phone number. This time he answered, sleepily.

'Tory? What's wrong? Can't sleep? Too busy thinking of me?' He laughed throatily. 'I was certainly thinking of you.'

Tory took a deep breath and started to speak. 'Damien,' she began, her nervousness evident even to her, 'I'm sorry, but I can't do today.' Her voice quivered and she couldn't stop it.

She heard a rustle as if he were sitting up in bed. 'Are you still feeling ill? I did warn you.'

She wouldn't let him believe she was just too ill to cook lunch; that would only be a short-term solution. 'No, it's not that.'

'Tory, what is it?' His voice was low; anxious. Did he sense what she was going to say?

'I think it's better if …' She closed her eyes as if she were in pain. 'If we don't see each other anymore.' The words erupted from her lips.

'What?' His tone was hurt and bewildered, all trace of amusement gone.

Tory swallowed, preparing to tell the lie that would sever them. 'It just won't work. I don't feel the same way, and it would be wrong of me to keep seeing you when I know it won't go anywhere.'

There was a long silence. 'I don't believe you,' he said at last.

'Believe me or not, that's no concern of mine. I thought it would be better to call it off now, before things go any further.' She bit her lip. This was far, far harder than she'd imagined it would be.

He was speechless, that was obvious. 'Well, thanks for letting me know,' he managed eventually. 'I guess I'll leave things at that. Wouldn't want to harass you when you're clearly not interested. Bye, Tory.'

And that was that. She cut the call and slowly laid the phone down on the bed. The bed that only yesterday had been a place of pleasure, of love even, and where she'd allowed herself to dream of a future with someone else.

Love? She gasped. Was she in love with him? Yes, she was. Finally, she admitted to herself what she'd known for a while, but refused to recognise: she was deeply in love, head over heels, drowning in it. And with that, she pressed her hands to her face and began to weep, hopelessly and despairingly, for all that she'd hoped for and now had to give up on.

★   ★   ★

'Mummy?' It was Millie walking into the room. 'Why are you crying?'

Tory looked at her daughter and saw the anxiety on her small face. 'I'm not crying, sweetie. I've got something in my eye, that's all.'

'When's Damien coming?'

'He's not. We've had to cancel.'

'No!' Millie shouted, stamping her dainty foot. 'Why? I wanted him to build another snowman with me. He promised.'

'I'm sorry, Millie. Shall we ring Auntie Julia and Megan to come instead? I'm sure Megan would love to build a snow-man with you.'

'Oh, all right, then.' The suggestion was very much a poor substitute in Millie's eyes. She pouted and frowned, and Tory knew then that she'd done the right thing in ending whatever was about to happen between her and Damien. Millie was starting to become as attached to him as Tory was.

'Okay, I'll ring Julia.'

★ ★ ★

Julia accepted immediately. 'I'm always happy to eat a meal cooked by someone else. What time?'

'Twelve?'

'Fine. See you then. I'll bring a bottle.'

The morning passed swiftly as Tory prepared a lavish roast dinner: lamb, roast potatoes, four different vegetables, and an apple pie for dessert. All the things she'd planned for Damien.

Julia took one look at Tory as she walked in and asked, 'What's wrong?'

The two children ran off upstairs to Millie's room without being asked, so

184

Tory poured them both a large glass of red wine and led the way into the sitting room. She told Julia what had happened between her and Damien, what Stuart had threatened the previous evening, and how she'd subsequently ended things with Damien.

'So as I understand it, you've let him believe you're just not interested at all?'

Tory took a huge gulp of her wine and nodded.

'And he believed you?' Julia cried in astonishment.

'Apparently.' Tory took another even larger mouthful. It seemed the only way to dull the pain she was experiencing. 'So it's over. I can't have him endangered. If Stuart really is crazy …'

'You're in love with Damien, aren't you?'

Tory nodded, tears stinging her eyes.

'And it looked to me as if he feels the same way about you. Tory, you can't let Stuart ruin your life. He's done enough of that already. You must go to the police.'

'What's the point? They've said they

can't do anything. They'd have to catch him in the act of threatening me. No, it's best if I steer clear of any other man. I've been thinking of moving on.'

'Don't you dare. He'd only find you again. And you can't spend your life running. The man's clearly obsessed. You need to call his bluff. I can't believe he'd seriously hurt anyone, let alone commit murder.'

'If you knew him like I do, you'd know he's perfectly capable of hurting someone.' Tears stung her eyes again. 'He hurt me badly enough.'

'Oh Tory, I'm so sorry. But there must be something you can do.'

She shrugged. 'If there is, I can't think of it.'

'Are you going to let him see Millie? Maybe that's all he wants, visitation rights? Maybe he could take her somewhere for a weekend?'

'No, never. I told you, if she didn't tidy her toys and put her clothes away in perfect order, he'd hit her — I know he would, Julia. He's obsessively controlling.

Everything has to be done his way, or else … I can't trust him with her.'

Tory put on a cheerful act in front of the two children over lunch, but that was all it was, an act. When the time came for Julia and Megan to leave, Julia asked, 'Are you going to work tomorrow?'

'I'll have to, or I risk losing my job. I'll bring Millie to you at the usual time.' It was nursery day on a Monday, so Millie would be safe there, at least. And Tory could go to work with an easy mind.

★   ★   ★

Tory and Millie spent a quiet evening, Tory reading aloud from one of Millie's favourite storybooks before putting her to bed. Despite having banished Damien from their lives, she couldn't help hoping he'd turn up on the doorstep. How, she repeatedly asked herself, could she have fallen in love so fast? So heedlessly? So foolishly?

Once Millie was in bed and asleep, Tory decided to have a long, hot bath, taking a large glass of wine with her, hoping the combined effects would help her sleep. Fortunately it worked, and she awoke the next morning refreshed and restored to her normal state of health, all ready to begin her day and drop Millie off at Julia's.

Julia greeted her warmly. 'You look back to normal. There's more colour in your cheeks. Any more problems?'

'No, we had a quiet evening and an early night. No sign of Stuart, and I haven't heard from him, so maybe he's realised his persecution of me isn't working and he's returned home.'

'Let's hope so,' Julia said grimly. 'Okay then, I'll see you later. Do you want me to bring Millie home for you?'

'No, I'll call in and fetch her.'

'Right. See you then. Hey, I've just had an idea. Do you fancy a night out tonight? It might take your mind off things. My neighbour, Rose, could come and babysit here for us.'

Tory regarded her doubtfully. 'I'd love to, but I'm not sure, not at the moment. Not with Stuart behaving like he's been.'

'Oh, come on. He wouldn't come here. And if he did, Rose would very quickly ring the police. I'll warn her not to open the door to anyone she doesn't know. You can't let him ruin things for you, Tory. That way he wins. Just for a couple of hours. Please?' she pleaded. 'I could do with some fun too. And you are entitled to a life.'

Tory was tempted, and Julia was right — Stuart was highly unlikely to turn up here. 'Well, okay, but only for a couple of hours. I wouldn't be happy staying any longer.'

'Fantastic.' Julia gave her a high-five. 'I'll sort it out with Rose. You might as well leave Millie with me after nursery. If you like, she can stay the night too.'

'I'm not sure about that. I don't think I want to be home alone. Pathetic, or what?' She gave a wry grin.

'Perfectly understandable. I'm sure I'd be the same. I'll drive so you can have a drink. I'll pick you up at seven.'

That evening, Tory changed out of her work clothes and donned a pair of jeans and a glitzy blouse and sat down to wait for Julia. As usual, she was early, so they were in The White Hart pub on the edge of Compton Cross by a little after seven, with the pick of the tables to sit at. They chose one immediately in front of a roaring log fire and ordered a bottle of red wine.

'What's the point of messing round with it by the glassful?' Julia said.

'Well, you are driving, Julia,' Tory pointed out.

'No worries. I can always leave the car here and we can ring for a taxi.'

With that, Tory began to relax, an exercise helped chiefly by her friend's infectious enjoyment. They were both well into their second glasses when Damien Grey walked in, accompanied by a woman who could have successfully modelled on a catwalk. She was enviably tall, five foot seven or eight, Tory estimated, with the sort of long blonde hair that looked as if it had been ironed, and a figure to die for. Some women had it all, and this one certainly did. No matter what Tory did with her own hair, it refused to stay tidy. That had been something else Stuart had constantly nagged her about.

'Uh-oh,' Julia groaned. 'What's he doing here? And with the world's most beautiful woman, to boot. Just when we were starting to enjoy ourselves.'

'It certainly didn't take him long to get over his disappointment with regards to me, did it?' muttered Tory.

Why on earth had she worried about hurting him? It looked as though he hadn't given Tory a second thought. She glared in his direction. It was unfortunate that he chose that particular moment to glance around the room, and of course he noticed her immediately. Tory, bolstered by her second glass of wine, cheekily raised her almost-empty glass in a mocking salute to him.

He stared, frozen momentarily, his brow pulled down into a frown. However he made a fast recovery, murmuring a few words to the woman at his side and then heading directly for Tory. Now it was her turn to freeze. Oh dear God. Now what?

'Oh no,' she wailed softly to Julia, 'he's coming over.'

'What are you two doing here?' were his first words, swiftly followed up with, 'Where's Millie?'

Tory stiffened. Was he implying she shouldn't have left her? 'I left her watching a horror movie on TV with some scissors and a box of matches for company. Where do you think she is?' she snapped.

'And what are you doing here?' Julia smartly asked. 'And,' she added, glancing beyond him towards his abandoned companion, 'who's the chick with you?'

Tory stared at her in astonishment. Chick? She almost laughed out loud.

'Oh, that's Cassandra. She's just a friend,' Damien told them smoothly, his gaze riveted on Tory.

'And Cassandra —' Tory deliberately emphasised the name. '— knows you regard her as just a friend, does she?'

'Of course. Not that it concerns you, one way or the other. Do you want to join us?'

'We're quite content, just the two of

us, thanks.'

'Well, as you're so contented in each other's company, I'll leave you to it. Nice to see you, Julia,' he went on, before turning back to Tory and coolly saying, 'Have a good evening.'

'And you,' Tory replied in deceptively honeyed tones.

'Oh, believe me, I intend to.' And he turned and strode back to the blonde.

Julia stuck her tongue out at his back, and she and Tory dissolved into almost hysterical giggles. From then on, Tory put on the act of her life: laughing, talking, and all the time acutely aware of Damien just a few metres away from her. He didn't as much as glance her way, and Tory felt more miserable with every second that passed, until at last he and Cassandra left.

'Okay,' Julia said, 'you can calm down now. Good act, though. Anyone would have thought you were having the time of your life, when in reality your heart was breaking, wasn't it?'

Tory nodded.

'I could tell. It's the eyes; they always give the game away.'

Tory hoped Damien hadn't seen the same thing. The last thing she wanted was for him to know how desperately unhappy she was. 'Would you mind if we went too, Julia? The evening's lost it gloss, somehow. I'm tired, plus I think I've had a bit too much to drink. How are you? Shall we ring for a taxi?'

'No, I'm fine. I've only had half a glass; you polished the rest of it off! Come on.'

★ ★ ★

Once back at Julia's, Tory carried a sleeping Millie out to the car, and her friend drove them back to Primrose Cottage. Tory nervously glanced around before getting out of the car, but to her relief there was no sign of Stuart. She quickly got them both into the house and carried Millie up to bed. The little girl hadn't stirred throughout.

That night, despite her exhaustion and the wine, Tory barely slept — and this time it wasn't due to her fear of

Stuart. Images of Damien and Cassandra plagued her. Was he still with her? Was he making love to her? She'd bet the stunning Cassandra wouldn't push him away and tell him she wasn't interested.

She tossed and turned, struggling to rid herself of her deep anguish, but it was no good. Eventually she got up and lit the log fire, sitting alongside it for what remained of the night.

The next couple of days passed with no disturbances of any sort. There'd been no sign of Stuart, so she'd gradually let herself believe he'd returned home. Maybe he needed to get back to work. He was a partner in the firm, after all.

There'd also been no sort of contact with Damien. Not that she'd expected any, not really. He'd been cold and distant in the pub, so he'd clearly put the interlude with her behind him and had found consolation elsewhere. And that really hurt. Had he meant any of the things he'd said to her?

Millie's day for nursery came round again, and Tory dropped her off at Julia's as usual on her way to work. The snow had all but gone, so it was easy to walk to work once again. No risk of slipping over and having to be picked up by a handsome man. Though she doubted, in Damien's case, whether he'd even bother to stop for her now, let alone pull her to her feet and drive her home.

As it happened, it was busy at the checkout, so the day passed quickly. Before she knew it, it was three-thirty. Not long now until home time, she told herself.

She was helping one of the other assistants to restock some shelves before they left, when the sound of her name being screamed rent the air. She swung to look and instantly registered Julia's ashen face. She ran to her.

'What? What's wrong? Tell me.' A terrible fear gripped her. Julia was bent double, panting, panic-stricken.

'Someone's taken Millie out of nursery.'

'What?' Tory grabbed Julia by the shoulders. 'What do you mean? Who? Who's taken her?' But she knew. It was

Stuart. Who else could it be?

'Miss Willis said a man who told her he was Millie's father turned up at two-thirty and said he needed to take her, as you'd been rushed to hospital — and as Millie had run to him, crying 'Daddy, Daddy,' she thought it was okay to let her go. Tory, it's Stuart. He's got her.'

Tory felt her head whirling dizzily. She swayed as her heart lurched with terror. 'He's done it,' she sobbed. 'He's snatched her. Oh, Julia.'

Her manager came over to them. 'Is something wrong, Mrs Matthieson? You're not ill again, are you? Because I have to say —'

'I have to go. It's my daughter. I have to go.'

'But you can't just leave —'

'It's an emergency.'

Tory and Julia raced out of the shop and across to Julia's car, which she'd parked illegally, half on the kerb and half on the road. 'I'll take you home,' she panted. 'Perhaps he's left a note or a letter for you. Or maybe he's there, waiting.'

'No, he can't get in — not since I had the lock changed. He might have left a note, though. He'll want me to know what he's done. He'll take enormous delight in that. He loves nothing more than hurting me. And he couldn't have chosen a better way. Oh, Millie, my precious baby.' The tears were brimming in her eyes. She mustn't break down; there was no time for that. The important thing now was to find her daughter. Nothing else mattered.

Julia drove back to the cottage, breaking all sorts of traffic laws. Tory was in a complete panic. She didn't know what to do first. Go to the police? Go after Stuart?

Once they reached the cottage, Tory raced inside. The first thing she saw was an envelope lying on the doormat. She grabbed it and ripped it open.

I've got Millie. You come back to our home, alone. No police, no friends, no family. If you don't do exactly as I say, I'll do to you what you did to me. I'll disappear with Millie, but I'll be cleverer than you and I'll do it properly. I'll be watching out for you, and if anyone's with you, I promise you'll never see Millie again.

Julia had appeared by the time she'd read it, Megan at her side. Tory thrust the single sheet at her. 'Read that.'

Julia gave a gasp of horror. 'He's bluffing. If he's in the house with Millie, how will he get her out if he sees someone's with you? You mustn't go alone.'

'I have to. He'll be watching from somewhere nearby, just as he's been doing here. I can't take the risk, Julia. I can't lose Millie — I can't.'

'Tory, the man's insane.'

'I have to protect Millie somehow. I can't be sure he won't hurt her, just to hurt me. If that means I return to Stuart, then so be it. I'll get away again. He can't be with me twenty-four hours a day. He has to work.'

'But he can hurt you while he's there. Listen to me. You took his daughter away from him and then wouldn't let him see her. He's hell-bent on revenge, that's perfectly clear from what he's written.'

199

She stared at Tory, her panic and deep concern written all over her face. 'Let me come with you. I can drop Megan off with Rose. I don't have to go to the house with you. I can wait somewhere, hidden. He won't know. You can ring me, or give some sort of signal, if you're in trouble. I could be there in moments.'

'No, Julia. It wouldn't work. You don't know him. I really believe he's capable of anything. I appreciate your offer, but I have to do this alone. I refuse to put anyone else in harm's way.' She gazed miserably into her friend's familiar face. 'Thank you for being such a wonderful friend. I don't know how I would have survived these past months — especially these past few weeks — without you.' She hugged Julia, the tears finally pouring from her eyes.

Julia clung to her, also weeping.

'Mummy, what's happening?' Megan was tugging at her mother's skirt. 'Why are you crying?'

Julia looked down at her distressed daughter. 'I'm sad because Tory and

Millie have to leave for a while.' She swung back to Tory. 'Ring me, please. Let me know you're okay. Wait; let me have your address.'

Tory picked up the pen that she always kept on the hall table and scribbled her address down on the back of the envelope that had contained Stuart's letter. 'I'll phone you as soon as I can.' She gave her friend one last hug and then tore herself away, unable to see clearly because of the tears still welling in her eyes.

She'd been so happy here up until these last few weeks, so free from fear. That was at an end. Now, who knew what the future held? Only misery and pain, she suspected. Even so, she had to go to Millie. The safety of her little girl was paramount.

12

Within minutes, Tory was on her way back to her old home and Stuart. She didn't have time to waste letting the estate agent know she would be terminating the rental agreement on the cottage. She'd write in a day or two and return the front door key. For now, her entire being was centred on finding and protecting Millie. Nothing else mattered. Nothing.

Her car, as small as it was, ate up the miles, and it was only an hour and a half later that she was pulling up in front of the house she'd left in such desperate haste just months ago. Stuart's car was parked on the driveway; he must be inside somewhere with Millie. Desperately trying to stem the terrible shaking that was threatening to shatter her into pieces, Tory climbed from the Fiesta and walked to the front door. She still had her door key, so she quietly let herself in. The first thing she heard was Millie's voice drifting down from her bedroom.

So Julia had been right. He had been bluffing. He hadn't had any intention of watching from a position nearby for her arrival. He was here. He'd been that confident she'd do as he'd ordered and come alone. What an idiot she'd been. She'd blindly walked into his trap. For a split second, she debated creeping from the house again and calling the police. But would they come, just on her say-so? The police in Compton Cross hadn't been very helpful. She listened carefully and heard Millie asking, 'When's Mummy going to come, Daddy? You said she'd be here.' Her voice was tearful; scared.

Stuart's response was curt and unmistakably conveyed his impatience; his total lack of understanding of the little girl's fears. 'I've told you, Millie, she'll be here soon. And if she isn't, well, we'll go off on an adventure. You'd like that, wouldn't you?'

Tory knew then she had no time to waste. Certainly no time to call for help.

She had to deal with this herself.

Swiftly and silently, she climbed the stairs and strode into her daughter's bedroom, for all the world as if she hadn't got a care in the world; as if her stomach wasn't heaving with fear and dread. 'I'm here, darling. I was delayed at work.'

Millie swung to her father, her expression one of accusation. 'You told a lie! You said Mummy was ill, in hospital, when she was at work.'

Stuart ignored the child as she ran to Tory and flung her arms around her mother's thighs. His gaze was firmly on his wife. He looked smug and triumphant. Tory bent and picked her small daughter up, hugging her.

'It's okay. Everything's okay.' She stared at her husband over Millie's head. 'Well, I'm here, so what now? What is it you want, Stuart?'

'I want us to be a family again. Is that so wrong? Is it too much to ask?'

He sounded as if he were pleading now, and although the smug expression was gone, Tory wasn't fooled. She knew his mood could change in a second, from complete calmness into a crazed and uncontrollable anger. 'It is, I'm afraid, and you know why.'

'In that case, put Millie down.' His face as well as his voice had hardened. Both were implacable; steely — a look and tone she'd been all too familiar with.

Tory did as he said. The last thing she wanted was for him to lose his temper and lash out at her while she was holding Millie.

'Okay.' He looked down at his small daughter. 'You stay here, Millie. I have to talk to Mummy.'

'But I want to come too, Daddy,' Millie whined.

'No.' Stuart barked out the single word. Millie's face crumpled and she began to whimper. Tory made a move towards her. 'And you stay just where you are. You've always spoilt her; given in to her. You're turning her into a brat. She's going to do as she's told from now on. I'll see to that.'

Millie looked outraged. 'I'm not a brat, am I, Mummy?' She bravely dashed her tears away, but couldn't quite stop the quivering of her bottom lip.

'No, darling, you're not,' Tory gently reassured her. 'You're a good girl, so do as Daddy says and stay here, will you?' A deep-seated dread was beginning within Tory.

Millie nodded her head. 'Okay, Mummy,' she whispered, not giving her father a single glance.

'Good. You're both learning,' Stuart retorted. 'Now, I'm going to close your door, Millie.'

Millie gave a muted groan of protest, but didn't say anything. Tory's heart ached for the little girl, but she knew she mustn't make a move towards her; mustn't provoke Stuart into any sort of retaliatory action.

He put his hand on her shoulder and pushed her from the room. She heard Millie whimper, 'Mummy …' as Stuart closed the door behind them. Then, Tory heard the sound of a bolt going across.

She glanced over her shoulder and saw it fixed onto the outside of the door.

'You don't have to lock her in. She'll be frightened. Stuart, please.'

He looked down at her, hatred twisting his features. '*Stuart, please*,' he mimicked her. 'Please what? Please don't hit me? You have to learn, Victoria, just as she does. My word is the only one that counts in this house, and that goes for my wishes, too. The sooner you accept that, the better it'll be for all of us. I will treat you exactly as I please.'

'I just don't want Millie upset. And if you hit me ...'

'Oh, well you won't have to concern yourself with that possibility. Since you left, I've had plenty of time to make a few alterations to the place. I've done up the cellar. I think you'll like it.'

And he smiled at her, a smile that despatched a chill right through her. He tightened his grip on her shoulder and forced her down the stairs. As they descended, he leant towards her and whispered in her ear. 'I've done it especially for you. It's completely soundproof, so you won't disturb anyone else. Come along.' He steered her to the door in the hall that led down into the underground room. That too had a bolt fitted on the outside. 'I'll show you.'

She stared at it in horror. 'Stuart?'

He ignored her and opened the door, shoving her through. It had only ever been used as a storeroom, for Stuart's collection of wines, chiefly. But a lot of the things that they hadn't used on a regular basis had been put down there. He switched on a light and pushed her down in front of him. The steep stairway was too narrow for two people to descend side by side. She staggered and almost fell.

'Be careful, darling,' he said smoothly as he grabbed hold of the back of her hair, pulling her backwards. She winced in pain. 'We don't want you falling down, do we?' His tone was honey-smooth; velvety, almost.

Tory began to tremble, her legs almost giving way beneath her.

'You'll be able to scream down here to your heart's content, my darling, and no one will hear you.'

'What?' She couldn't believe what she was hearing. 'Stuart, you can't. Please, don't do this, please.'

'Oh, don't whine,' he sneered. 'I can't stand women who whine, and you certainly did plenty of that.'

Tory wondered then how she could ever have believed she loved him. He was loathsome; repellent. Vicious.

They reached the bottom step and he turned on another light. She gasped. He'd transformed the space into a bedroom. There was a single bed and a chair, and that was all. It was a cell: monastic, stark, with a concrete floor and bare stone walls. Everything else had been removed.

'You should be comfortable here.'

She swung to face him. He smiled; a smile that didn't reach his eyes. They remained cold, unblinking; reptilian. Julia was right — he was insane, and perfectly capable of keeping her prisoner.

'You can't keep me down here. People will notice I'm not around.'

He cocked his head at her. 'Will they?

You haven't been around for months. Why would they miss you or wonder where you are?'

'My car's outside.'

'Oh, that can easily be sorted,' he scoffed. 'I'll dump it somewhere. Maybe sell it. No one will be any the wiser. Now, take your coat off.'

Fear overwhelmed her then; a fear like nothing she'd ever experienced before. In her urgent haste to get to Millie, she'd walked into a deadly trap; one she had no chance of escaping from. But how could she have imagined he'd go this far?

In a bid to keep him calm, she did as he said. 'What about Millie?' she asked. 'She'll want to know where I am.'

'I'll tell her you've left us. Cruel mummy.' He pulled a mocking face. 'Deserting her little girl. She's young; she'll believe whatever I tell her.'

'Stuart, I'll do whatever you want, but please don't do that to Millie. She'll be heartbroken.'

'For a while, maybe.' He shrugged. 'She'll soon forget. Children do.'

'And what about my parents? Bella?'

'I'll tell them the same. You sent Millie back to me and went off with a man. Oh yes, Damien Grey.' He regarded her, his expression one of utter contempt. 'Did you think I wouldn't realise what was going on with him? Do I look stupid?'

'Nothing's going on with him. I haven't seen him in days. He was just a friend. He isn't even that any longer.'

He snorted. 'Yeah, right.'

'It's true.' But it was hopeless. He wasn't going to believe a single word she said. He'd made up his mind about her and Damien and nothing was going to change that. Still, she had to try, for Millie's sake. She'd do anything to save her daughter from this madman.

'Stuart, you want to be a family again. You said so. We can be —'

'He rejected you, didn't he?' His eyes narrowed to slits. 'Well, it doesn't matter what you say now. You're not leaving me again. You've left me with no alternative.'

Tory felt tears brim in her eyes.

'Oh, don't start snivelling. You go off

without a word, take my daughter away from me, refuse to let me see her — you deserve to be punished.' He raised his hand and slapped her, hard, across her face.

She staggered backwards and fell onto the floor, banging her head in the process. She groaned and lifted a hand up to the back of her head. She felt the wetness of blood. Her lip stung, so she gently touched that too. When she looked at her fingers, she saw they were covered with blood.

Truly terrified now, she used her elbows to try and drag herself backwards across the floor. If she could just reach the stairs, maybe she could run up. But in the next second, he was on her. He dragged her upright and then across to the bed, and heaved her onto it.

'No one runs away from me. You're my wife.' Instinctively, she cowered back as he thrust his face almost into hers. She could feel his hot breath on her skin; see the hatred in his eyes. His fingers bit into the tops of her arms as he began to violently shake her. 'You belong to me. Understand? And I'll treat you as I see fit.' He lifted a hand and slapped her again.

Suddenly, there was a loud banging on the front door. In his haste to get her down the stairs and into her prison cell, Stuart had forgotten to close the cellar door behind them.

'Mr Matthieson? Police. Open up. Mr Matthieson. Open the door, please.'

Stuart froze. Then Tory heard the sounds of splintering wood and the noise of many feet.

'Mrs Matthieson? Are you here? Tell us where you are.'

'Down here!' she screamed. 'In the cellar!'

She looked at Stuart. He was a man transformed. His face went grey as he seemed to shrink before her very eyes. She tore herself away from him and ran for the stairs, just as several policemen leapt down towards her. Then, unbelievably, she saw Damien right behind them. One of the policemen put out an arm to try and stop him from running forward.

'Sir, stop. Stay back.'

'I'm the one who phoned you and told you to come here. Now, let me through.'

He pushed past the policemen and strode directly to Tory, then reached for her with both arms. She collapsed into them, sobbing as much with relief as with the pain that Stuart had inflicted. Behind her she heard one of the policemen reading Stuart his rights, then she heard the click of handcuffs being fastened, and he was being hauled past her and up the cellar stairs.

'Millie,' Tory gasped. 'My daughter. He's locked her in her bedroom.'

'I'll get her, Mrs Matthieson,' she heard someone say, and one of the uniformed men ran up the stairs.

Damien then held her away from him, horrified as he studied the bruises that were beginning to form on her face, and the bleeding lip. 'Tory. Are you able to walk?'

She nodded.

'Okay, let's get you upstairs then.' And he tenderly led her away.

Eventually, when the police had all their statements, and photographic evidence of Stuart's handiwork on the house and Tory's injuries, they left.

Millie stared at her mother, taking in her bleeding mouth and bruised face, before asking in a wobbly little voice, 'Did Daddy do that to you?'

'He did, darling. Daddy's very ill.'

'I don't like Daddy anymore,' Millie said tearfully. 'Will I have to see him?'

'No, sweetheart, you won't.'

Damien took them both to hospital. It took some time, but once they'd been checked over and pronounced fit enough to go, he turned to Millie and said, 'Back to Primrose Cottage?' He then looked at Tory and raised an eyebrow at her, mutely asking the same question.

'Yes, please,' she said gratefully.

'We'll go in my car,' he told her. 'You're in no fit state to drive. We'll get yours collected in a day or two.'

Tory didn't argue. He was right; she was far too shaky to handle a car.

As Damien drove, he told her how

Julia had managed to get hold of him on the phone minutes after Tory had gone and told him all that had happened. How Tory had been systematically beaten and abused until, fearful for her life and Millie's safety, she'd run away. How Stuart had been stalking her, terrorising her, finally snatching Millie and threatening to disappear with her if Tory didn't return to him. She finished by saying that Tory was now, in her opinion, in very serious danger. She'd given him her friend's address, and he'd set off at once. He'd notified the local police and set in motion Tory and Millie's rescue.

'I think you should ring her, if you feel up to it,' Damien said.

'Without Julia's swift action, he'd probably have killed you. And I know how frightened she was for you.'

Tory didn't hesitate. She dialled her friend's number. Julia answered on the second ring. 'Oh, Tory — thank God. Damien found you.'

'Just in time,' Tory told her, her voice

shaking with emotion. 'I can't thank you enough.'

'It's not me you need to thank, it's Damien. He didn't hesitate, Tory — he loves you. If you could've seen the way he looked when I told him what had been happening ...'

'I know,' Tory quietly answered, sliding her glance towards him now. He smiled at her, his eyes tender and filled with love — just as Julia said. 'I'll speak to you later, when we're home. Thanks, Julia. I'll never forget what you've done.'

'I should damn well hope not,' Julia robustly said with her customary irreverence. 'It certainly deserves a drink or three.'

'You'll have them,' Tory laughed — slightly shakily, but laugh she did. 'Damien,' she then said, turning to the man at her side, 'I don't know what to say. After the way I treated you — I feel so bad about that.'

'Yeah, well,' he said, 'Julia explained that, too. You could've told me the truth, you know. I knew something wasn't right;

I just couldn't put my finger on what. I was actually on the verge of coming to see you, to try and find out what was really going on, when Julia phoned me.'

She stared at him. 'I didn't want to burden anyone else with my problems. And I didn't want anyone else getting involved. Getting hurt.'

He returned her gaze, his look one of deep tenderness. 'I love you, Tory. I have from the first time I saw you lying there on the pavement. I just wanted to pick you up and hold you. But you were so prickly, so defiant, so damned determined not to appear helpless.' He grinned. 'And as for Millie, I fell for her just as quickly. You're both utterly irresistible.'

For a long moment, Tory couldn't speak. She watched as an expression of despair appeared within Damien's eyes. He believed she was about to say she didn't return his feelings.

'I love you as well,' she softly told him. 'And Millie adores you.'

A look of unutterable happiness came

over him. 'Thank God for that. Right — home, now.'

He held out a hand to her. She took it and gave a sigh of pure happiness. She was going home, somewhere she'd truly believed at one point she'd never see again. And, what was more, it would be with the man she loved. She couldn't wait.

* * *

When they reached the cottage, Damien gently lifted a sleeping Millie from the car and carried her up to her bedroom, where he laid her on her bed, still dressed, and covered her with her quilt. He then stood, looking down on the small girl, before turning to gaze at Tory. She held out her hand to him. He took it and she led him into her own bedroom.

'Tory?' he said uncertainly.

He didn't have to speak the words. She knew exactly what he was asking her. 'I'm sure.'

'Because I can wait …'

'Can you?' She looked at him, her love

for him transparently clear upon her bruised face. 'Well, I can't.'

He stood quite still, his gaze searching hers intently, before he took a single stride towards her and took her into his arms. She pulled his head towards her and pressed her lips to his.

'Mummy, Mummy ...'

Damien leapt back. 'Oh, Jees!'

Tory began to laugh. 'As I believe I pointed out once before under similar circumstances, this is one of the joys of parenthood.'

He grinned back, that devilishly attractive grin that she loved so very much. 'I can put up with that. You stay here. It'll be my pleasure to go.'

And, astonishingly, he did.

She heard Millie cry, 'Damien, I'm so glad you're here. Are you going to take care of me and Mummy from now on?'

And when she heard Damien say, 'I most certainly am,' she knew she'd truly come home.

We do hope that you have enjoyed reading this large print book.

Did you know that all of our titles are available for purchase?

We publish a wide range of high quality large print books including:
Romances, Mysteries, Classics
General Fiction
Non Fiction and Westerns

Special interest titles available in large print are:
The Little Oxford Dictionary
Music Book, Song Book
Hymn Book, Service Book

Also available from us courtesy of Oxford University Press:
Young Readers' Dictionary
(large print edition)
Young Readers' Thesaurus
(large print edition)

For further information or a free brochure, please contact us at:
Ulverscroft Large Print Books Ltd.,
The Green, Bradgate Road, Anstey,
Leicester, LE7 7FU, England.
Tel: (00 44) **0116 236 4325**
Fax: (00 44) **0116 234 0205**

PALACE OF DECEPTION

Helena Fairfax

When a Mediterranean princess disappears with just weeks to go before her investiture, Lizzie Smith takes on the acting role of her life — she is to impersonate Princess Charlotte so that the ceremony can go ahead. As Lizzie immerses herself in preparation, her only confidante is Léon, her quiet bodyguard. In the glamorous setting of the Palace of Montverrier, Lizzie begins to fall for Léon. But what secrets is he keeping from her? And who can she really trust?

SHADOWS AT BOWERLY HALL

Carol MacLean

Forced to work as a governess after the death of her father, Amelia Thorne travels north to Yorkshire and the isolated Bowerly Hall. Charles, Viscount Bowerly, is a darkly brooding employer, and Amelia is soon convinced that the stately home hold secrets and danger in its shadows. Then a spate of burglaries in the county raises tensions amongst the villagers and servants, and Amelia finds herself on the hunt for the culprit. Can Charles be trusted?

SUMMER'S DREAM

Jean M. Long

Talented designer Juliet Croft is devastated when the company she works for closes. She takes a temporary job at the Linden Manor Hotel, but soon hears rumours that the business is in financial difficulties — and suspects that Sheldon's, a rival company, is involved. During her work, she renews her friendship with Scott, a former colleague. At the same time, she must cope with her growing feelings for Martin Glover, the hotel manager. Trouble is, he's already taken . . .

SEEING SHADOWS

Susan Udy

Lexie Brookes is busy running her hairdressing salon and wondering what to do about her cooling relationship with her partner, Danny. When the jewellery shop next door is broken into via her own premises, the owner — the wealthy and infuriatingly arrogant Bruno Cavendish — blames her for his losses. Then Danny disappears, and Lexie is suddenly targeted by a mysterious stalker. To add to the turmoil, Bruno appears to be attracted to her, and she finds herself equally drawn to him . . .